THE SLAUGHTERED WIDOW

Bailiff Mountsorrel Mysteries
Book Three

David Field

SAPERE
BOOKS

THE SLAUGHTERED WIDOW

Published by Sapere Books.

24 Trafalgar Road, Ilkley, LS29 8HH,
United Kingdom

saperebooks.com

ISBN: 978-0-85495-357-8

1

Nottingham, 1593

Edward Mountsorrel, bailiff to the Sheriff of Nottinghamshire, stood grim-faced at the back of a small crowd that had assembled in the upper chamber of Nottingham's Guildhall. They were there to learn whether or not the presenting jury would commit, for trial, the man sitting in manacles and charged with murder. Having heard what passed for evidence in the case — most of which Edward found impossible to believe — he was hardly surprised when, without even withdrawing to consider the matter, the lead juror announced that they had found a 'true bill', meaning that they believed the accused to be guilty.

Magistrate Charles Plowright announced that the prisoner was to be kept confined in the cells below the Guildhall to await trial at the next available assize, charged with the murder of Agnes Timberlake. The shackles that had been around the prisoner's feet for the hearing were unlocked and he was hauled to his feet and led down through the hatch to the cell beneath. As he passed out of sight the committed man looked across at Edward, and shook his head as if in resignation of his fate.

Edward swore bitterly. The prisoner was his friend and colleague, Francis Barton, and, if Edward were honest with himself, his *only* friend these past few years. Francis was accused of a murder that he almost certainly did not commit, yet the evidence against him was both clear and convincing. The murdered woman had been Francis's lover, and Edward could not bring himself to believe that such a brutal death could have been at the hands of the bailiff to the Sheriff of Nottingham.

An hour later, Edward ducked under the lintel at the front door of the house he occupied with his wife Elizabeth and their one-year-old daughter Margaret, named after Edward's mother, with whom he had been briefly reunited after many years of believing himself to have been an abandoned orphan. He and Francis had unearthed a nest of plotters against Queen Elizabeth's crown and Edward's mother had been callously murdered in an act of revenge. Francis had set off after the person believed to have been responsible and had returned to assure Edward that the man was dead. Francis had proved his friendship for Edward, and Edward was not about to abandon him now in his hour of need.

'I need not ask how matters transpired,' Elizabeth said, after kissing Edward warmly on the lips. 'I can see it in your face. But I hope that it has not diminished your appetite for dinner.'

Edward smiled and shook his head. 'Nothing will deter me from enjoying one of Meg's fine roasts. How is Margaret?'

'She's sleeping, finally,' Elizabeth said.

A few minutes later Edward sighed as he carved another slice from the roast with his eating knife. 'I wish that we could take some of this to Francis, since he'll be lucky to get a slice of stale bread and a mug of water from the Leen that someone has already pissed in.'

'They wouldn't do that to one of their own, surely?' Elizabeth asked.

Edward shrugged. 'I would not discount that possibility. Francis can be very hard on his constables and turnkeys when the occasion merits. But hopefully they'll take pity on a man confined in one of his own cells.'

'Is there no hope that he might be granted his bail?'

Edward shook his head. 'For one thing, the evidence against Francis seems very strong, and if I did not know him better I too would be convinced of his guilt. There is also the fact that the charge is almost as serious as it could be. But more to the point, the magistrate is Charles Plowright, whose wealth comes from supplying ale to most of the lower drinking dens in the town towards which Francis and his constables have in recent years given close attention. Every alehouse that Francis closed, even temporarily, resulted in a reduction in Plowright's fortune. He has more than once complained to Sheriff Drury that he is being singled out for persecution, so he will see this as his God-given opportunity to get his revenge on Francis.'

'How will the town manage while Francis is in the cells at the Guildhall?' Elizabeth asked.

Edward grimaced. 'I think I got an inkling of that this morning when it fell to Sheriff Drury to produce the evidence against Francis, his own bailiff no less. His face when he did so resembled a tub of sour lemons, and he took me to one side before the proceedings commenced and bid me attend at his dwelling after I have dined.'

'Do you think that he too believes Francis to be innocent of the charge?'

'I think it more likely that he felt embarrassed that the man he was presenting was one who has, since he became sheriff a few months ago, been responsible for collecting the evidence against other wrongdoers. When Francis goes to trial at the next assize, he will be in a list containing others accused of crime thanks to his efforts in unmasking their misdeeds. No doubt I shall learn more when I present myself as demanded. Wish me good fortune in that regard.'

An hour later Edward slipped from the saddle and handed his horse's bridle to a groom, who led it towards the stable at the rear of the Wheeler Gate home of the new Sheriff of Nottingham, Thomas Drury. Announcing his arrival to the steward, he was admitted into the sitting room. Edward suppressed a groan as two men rose from their chairs by the empty fireplace and he recognised the bulky figure of his own employer, Sir Francis Willoughby, Sheriff of Nottinghamshire, now enjoying his third term of office.

Edward and Sir Francis were connected in another way. Edward's wife Elizabeth had been employed as lady's maid to Willoughby's daughter, Lady Bridget. Willoughby had not approved of Edward and Elizabeth's courtship, but the sheriff had grudgingly accepted a working relationship with Edward after Queen Elizabeth herself had intervened on their behalf.

Thomas Drury held out his hand and inclined his head towards Willoughby. 'You are no doubt wondering why Sir Francis has joined us this afternoon?'

'I can only assume that it has something to do with my immediate duties?' Edward replied diplomatically.

Drury nodded. 'Yes, it does, and I am most grateful to him for loaning the town your services.'

'I am no longer employed in the county?' Edward asked in surprise.

'Both at the same time,' Drury hastened to explain. 'You will, of course, have realised that until matters have taken their course in this unfortunate matter involving Master Barton, there will be no bailiff available to serve the town.'

'Do you not, as do I, believe him to be innocent?' Edward asked.

Drury's expression hardened slightly. 'What I believe is neither here nor there, which is perhaps as well, given that it falls to me to prosecute the matter in my official capacity. What *is* beyond doubt is that the town is currently without a bailiff, and I cannot appoint a substitute while this dreadful charge is hanging over the head of the current incumbent. I therefore require you to assume overall responsibility for the town. I appreciate that you will only be required to do so on a part-time basis, given your duties in the county.'

Edward looked in Willoughby's direction as he asked, 'Presumably, Sir Francis has given his consent to such an arrangement?'

'I have indeed,' Willoughby confirmed, 'since I believe you are capable of shouldering the additional burden, and that your current investigations at county level will permit the same.'

Edward frowned. 'It was barely a week ago that you set me to identifying those who have been burglarising the houses of the wealthy in the outlying villages to the north of town. I have yet to complete those enquiries, and it will be to the detriment of both the county and my reputation if I am to be distracted by the need to suppress the crime and disorder of this town.'

'Hopefully this temporary arrangement will not remain for long,' Drury replied. 'The next assize is barely a few weeks away and then we shall know Barton's fate one way or the other. If he hangs, then I can go in search of a replacement, but if he is acquitted, then he may resume his former duties.'

'At present I know little of this matter,' Willoughby said. 'Perhaps you might give me some knowledge of the case against your man, in order that I might assess for myself the likely length of this temporary arrangement?'

Drury duly obliged. 'I confess myself to be torn between my official duty to present facts, which, were it any other man, I would have no doubt speak eloquently of his guilt, and my reluctance to believe that such a dedicated officer of the law could have brought himself to such a pass.'

'My sentiments entirely,' Edward chimed in, to a disapproving frown from both sheriffs.

'Your sentiments count for nothing in this, Master Mountsorrel,' Drury reminded him, 'and you should not allow your association with the accused man to cloud your judgement, any more than have I.'

'The facts?' Willoughby prompted him, and Drury nodded as he outlined them.

'The murdered woman was one Agnes Timberlake, a widow in her middle years of life. She resided in Cow Lane, which lies adjacent to the old town wall to the north. Her husband, Thomas, had been one of the town's most successful and prominent merchants of the alabaster statues for which Nottingham enjoys a fine reputation. When he died, he left the widow not only the family home but also a substantial sum of money, believed to have been in excess of a thousand pounds. The son of the marriage, also named Thomas, continues the enterprise from a workshop adjacent to the house, where he had occasion in recent years to note the comings and goings of Master Barton, who is widely reputed to have been in a long-standing relationship with the widow.'

'Francis has made no secret of that relationship,' Edward interjected, only to be ignored by both men as Drury continued.

'On the evening of the fifth of July this year, Thomas was invited to supper with his mother. He resides in his own dwelling off Linby Lane, but he has a key to the house in Cow

Lane. On this occasion he had not brought the key with him, being of the belief that the house would be opened for him either by his mother, or by the family servant, Mary. It transpired, however, that Mary had been given the afternoon off while her mistress entertained Master Barton. Thomas Timberlake, when he arrived, found the door locked against him, and made considerable noise in the hope of attracting his mother to the door in order to open it to him. When this proved unsuccessful, and in the belief that some ill fate might have befallen her, he prevailed upon certain neighbours to assist him in breaking down the door.'

'Could he not gain access by way of the adjacent workshop?' Edward asked.

Drury frowned. 'This sorry tale will never be completed if you keep interrupting.'

Edward mumbled his apology.

'When entry was eventually gained to the house, it was to the sight of Agnes Timberlake lying naked in her bed, covered in her own life's blood, and with hideous wounds to the upper part of her exposed body. Standing in the room was Master Barton, his hose drenched in the widow's blood, and his sword lying at the side of the bolster, also blood-smeared. He could not account for what had happened, and the constables were called. Barton was consigned to his own cells while enquiries were conducted, which revealed not only the carnal relationship between the accused man and the dead woman, but also the telling fact that some years previously the widow had loaned her entire fortune, in the form of gold lodged in the vaults of a local merchant, to Barton for the remainder of her life, for him to make such use of it as he saw fit. It was seemingly to be repaid upon her death.'

'Why, pray, would Francis murder the woman, if it would result in his having to repay the loan?' Edward asked.

Drury raised a hand in the air to silence him. 'You seem too eager to exonerate your friend, Master Mountsorrel. Further enquiries of the merchant in whose vaults the gold had been consigned revealed that in recent months Agnes Timberlake had made frequent requests of Barton for the return of the loaned money, which she wanted to use to expand the workshop and thereby enable her son to take on more employees. Barton had been resisting these demands, and had insisted on the term of the loan agreement that did not require repayment until the widow's death. It is believed that they argued further on that issue on the day of her death, and that Barton lost control of his emotions and ran her through with his sword.'

'Thus bringing about the very result that, according to you, he was seeking to avoid,' Edward said. 'Your case has a fatal weakness!'

'I merely state the known facts,' Drury asserted, stern-faced. 'The conclusions to be drawn from the facts are for the assize jury, and not for either you or I.'

'But no-one has sought to look behind or beyond such facts as have been disclosed,' Edward pressed. 'And has anyone asked Francis himself for an explanation of those facts?'

'Why would that be done?' Drury asked.

Edward looked askance at both sheriffs. 'Because we might then learn more about the matter,' he pointed out, appalled that neither sheriff seemed to regard that as important in the case.

Drury's eyes narrowed. 'Our task is simply to provide such facts to the court as are sufficient to justify a presentment by the grand jury, and a conviction by those called upon to assess guilt at the resulting assize.'

'If we are to pursue such efficiency in the matter of putting a man on trial for his life,' Edward said coldly, 'that we merely present those facts that speak of his guilt, then why do we not save even more time by dispensing with any trial, and simply trundling the accused man on the back of a cart direct to Gallows Hill?'

The sheriffs stared back in the face of such an outrageous proposal, but it was Willoughby who spoke for them both. 'You propose to make yourself into some sort of representative for your friend? How will that detract from your efficient discharge of your double duties?'

'I care not how much it affects the discharge of my duties,' Edward replied defiantly as he rose to leave. 'Rest assured that I shall devote all the hours necessary to bring to justice those who are guilty, in addition to generating as much paper as your offices require in the matter of revenue collection and gaol records. But I shall also set about ensuring that Francis Barton has at his disposal *all* the facts pertinent to this matter. I was not of the belief that he might be allocated someone to help defend him in his cause. However, I would appear to be the closest that he is ever likely to be vouchsafed in that regard, so you will, I hope, forgive me if I make an early departure in order to discharge so many duties at once.'

Edward swirled his cloak over his shoulder and strode from the chamber, his riding boots striking hollowly against the wooden floor at the edge of the carpet as he reached the door, wrenched it open, and slammed it behind him.

2

Edward entered the Guildhall and walked through the Bailiff's Office, the Constables' Duty Room and the Turnkey Station until he came to a halt in front of the battered desk of Senior Constable Shanahan.

'Good evening, Patrick,' Edward breezed informally. 'Why are you still here? It will soon be dark and if you're still on duty, then your place lies out on the streets, scooping up offenders as swiftly as they offend, does it not?' Shanahan remained silent.

'Is it not the case that you were waiting to see if I'd show my face in here so soon after being given my new instructions?' Edward persisted. 'Who exactly tipped you off regarding the temporary arrangement, since I myself was only advised of it this afternoon?'

'Sheriff Drury, sir,' Shanahan replied, red-faced. 'But I wasn't waiting to see if you'd show up — I was just about to give the men their instructions for the night, then I was thinking about going home.'

'So they're still here somewhere, are they?' Edward replied. 'Get them in here now, because I have something to say to them.'

Five minutes later Edward had the undivided attention of four town constables whose task it would be to keep the lid down on potentially riotous and unseemly misbehaviour during the hours before nine the following morning. Shanahan effected the introductions and Edward wasted no more time as he let his gaze drift across each of their faces while addressing them.

'I need not refer to the unfortunate event that has left me in temporary command of the town. Suffice it to say that I shall be undertaking responsibilities for all matters in both jurisdictions. Thus, while I shall, for the time being, be your most senior commander in respect of matters that arise in the town proper, I shall continue to engage in matters that concern the county. But, as Bailiff Barton and myself discovered to our mutual advantage, problems encountered in the county frequently find their solutions in the town, and as you go about your various duties I wish you to be alert to those who have unaccountably, and unusually, come into possession of unaccustomed wealth. Put more plainly, if you learn of those of a lowly station in life making use of a higher class of town prostitute, or being uncharacteristically generous in buying drinks for their associates, then I require their names, and — if you can think of good reason — their presence in the cells downstairs, where I may enquire of them as to the source of their new-found riches.'

'What is it they are suspected of, sir?' asked one alert constable.

'There has of late been a series of burglaries from the houses in villages to the north of here such as Basford and Arnold. The items stolen were, in the main, of high value, and will have generated a pretty penny for those responsible for their theft. So enquire also in those premises that you know to be the usual depositories of thieves. The bell-brows of jackdaws known to offer low prices for items of high value. Thieves cannot operate without those prepared to buy from them at discounted rates, so look well about you as you progress through the town. In return for that I shall be investigating more fully into the circumstances that have led to Bailiff Barton being a guest in his own gaol, and should I require any assistance in that regard I have little doubt that you will supply it willingly. And so, please go about your duties, once Master Shanahan has allocated your beats.'

Leaving the senior constable to organise his men, Edward walked back to the Turnkey Station, which was cramped, with a low ceiling that forced men of Edward's height into a cautious stoop if they were to avoid hitting their heads on the ceiling beams. Senior Turnkey Will Possett was sitting behind the desk, poring over some paperwork, and looked up apprehensively as Edward entered.

'If those are the monthly records, you may hand them to me,' Edward told Possett with an air of authority. He had not forgotten the last occasion they had met, when one of Possett's men had allowed a man to escape from custody below the Shire Hall. Despite what ought by rights to have resulted in his dismissal, Bailiff Barton had taken pity on Possett and allowed him to retain not only his position but also his rank, by persuading Edward to transfer him from the Shire Hall to the Guildhall. As Possett gathered the papers together, Edward said, 'You will no doubt recall the circumstances in which we last met?'

Possett's gaze fell to his desk. 'Yes, sir — an' I said I were sorry then, an' I'm *still* sorry.'

'So how are you demonstrating your gratitude to Bailiff Barton, now that he has fallen on barren times and is one of your prisoners below?'

'I see to it that 'e gets fed proper and regular, sir.'

'Once a day? Bread and water?'

'Yes, sir — like all the rest.'

'But he *isn't* like all the rest, is he?' Edward challenged him. 'He's your benefactor, and — if everyone has their rights and the truth be told — he will shortly be your superior again, will he not?'

'Yes, sir.'

'So you perhaps owe it to him to ensure that he is fed at least twice a day.'

'Yes, sir.'

'And that he receives visits, whenever required, by the man who intends to work tirelessly to ensure that he does not hang? We understand each other, do we not?'

'Yes, sir. Do you want to see him right now?'

Five minutes later Edward was admitted through a heavy oak door that was closed diplomatically once he was inside the narrow dank cell. Possett had placed a rush torch halfway up the wall of the cell for their convenience and in the dancing shadows Edward could see Francis huddled in a corner on a straw-filled palliasse that constituted his bedding.

'I would rise and shake your hand, except that I stink too greatly,' Francis mumbled in a downcast voice.

Edward's heart went out to him, and he lost no time in recounting the conversation he'd recently had with Possett.

Francis managed a half smile. 'I thank you for a kindness that I do not perhaps deserve. You are seeking to lighten the wretched remaining days of a man fit only to hang.'

'Fie!' Edward replied sharply, appalled to hear his usually jocular friend so downcast and seemingly resigned to his fate. 'I am sworn to prove your innocence.'

Francis looked back up at him through hollow eyes. 'If even I cannot convince myself of my innocence, what chance have I of persuading either you or a jury?'

'You believe yourself to be guilty?' Edward demanded, appalled.

Francis shrugged. 'In truth, I have no way of knowing, Edward. I have no memory of what transpired between Agnes and myself, and I cannot discount the possibility that I did that of which I stand accused.'

'I know you better than that, Francis Barton,' Edward insisted in a stern voice. 'Not only are you incapable of so cowardly a deed, but you loved the woman, did you not?'

'Deeply,' Francis confirmed in a voice laden with terrible sadness. 'I cannot imagine how it could have come about, but we *had* been arguing sometime earlier, and it may be that a sudden anger overcame me of which I now have no conscious memory.'

'Then answer me this,' Edward insisted. 'How came it that when found dead, she was naked?' Francis appeared to blush, although it was difficult to tell in the half light from the rush torch.

'If truth be told, we were just about to make love as usual.'

'So you remember that at least?' Edward pressed him. 'You argued earlier that day, then you decided to make love, was that the way of it? Then if so, how could so much anger have returned to cause you to inflict such grievous injuries on a woman with whom you were about to become so intimate?'

Francis shook his head. 'I know not. I cannot remember anything beyond the two of us disrobing in her bedchamber, and the next thing I was rising to go to the jakes in the back garden, stumbling to put on my hose, and the evidence of what I must have done lay all around me. There was a commotion at the front door, and then men raced into the chamber to see only too clearly what had transpired.'

'How did you become aware that Agnes was dead?'

'When I looked back into the bed, she was … covered … from head to foot. Oh, God help me, it is a sight I shall never forget!'

Edward had never seen Francis so overcome, and he gave him a moment before asking, 'And your sword?'

'It was lying by the side of the bolster. I immediately checked my own belt, only to find that my sword was missing from it.'

'Did you take any steps to confirm that the sword lying by the bolster was indeed yours?'

'Not at that moment, since as I already mentioned there was a commotion by the front door. Then three men ran into the chamber, saw what had happened and picked up the sword from the floor. I was asked if it was mine, and I had to confess that it was, since it has my initials embossed on the hilt. It was a gift from the previous bailiff when he retired and I took over his office.' Francis gave a long moan. 'That I should have brought such disgrace upon such an honourable calling!'

'We do not know for certain that you have,' Edward reminded him. 'If it is not too painful, please recall what you can of everything that transpired that day.'

Francis appeared to be deep in thought as he went over the events of the fateful day. 'I was invited to supper with Agnes and her son Thomas, to discuss certain matters that had caused dissent between them. I believe that Agnes was seeking my support for her refusal to advance any of the family inheritance to Thomas, given his dissolute ways. Agnes asked that I arrive well ahead of the supper hour, in order that we might withdraw to her chamber for —' Francis coughed — 'well, you know. The girl Mary served us wine, and was then dismissed for the remainder of the afternoon, with orders to come back in order to serve the supper.'

'Did this not strike you as unusual — for Agnes to dismiss the servant girl while she was entertaining a guest?'

'That was her normal practice on days when I visited,' Francis explained, 'since she did not wish our activities in the chamber to become a source of local gossip. I advised her that we were already the talk of half the town, but she still insisted that we be alone. And so she dismissed the girl as normal, and we were alone in the house.'

'How can you be certain that Mary actually left the house, and that no-one else entered it while you were otherwise engaged?'

'I distinctly recall Mary leaving the house and Agnes securing the back door that leads to the garden, with its kitchen and jakes. Then she locked both the front door and the door that leads to the workshop where Thomas conducts the family business. So you see, we were entirely alone, and no-one could have entered while we were upstairs in the bedchamber.'

'Unless they had a key of their own,' Edward pointed out. 'Who had such keys?'

'I know not,' Francis admitted with a shake of the head. 'I believe that Thomas has keys to all the doors in the house, including the adjoining one to the workshop, but Agnes made a special point of leaving the key in the lock of the workshop door, so that neither Thomas nor anyone else could enter by that door, even had they a key.'

'Tell me more about the son, Thomas,' Edward said. 'You mentioned a certain discussion with his mother?'

Francis nodded. 'There was an argument as to whether or not Agnes should continue to resist her son's constant demands for money that he might squander away. Agnes had been left a fortune when she became a widow, and since Thomas was able to provide for himself from the business that he had inherited, Agnes opted to leave her money — in the form of gold — in the vaults of a local merchant called Josiah Greenwood. He owns a warehouse in Goose Gate, from which he sells farming tools, seed and the like, and to that end has a secure vault in his basement, to which he gives access to the more well-to-do townsfolk, for the safe storage of their wealth. His fees in that regard are modest, but he does such a brisk business that it is reckoned that the income therefrom exceeds what he enjoys from his regular merchant activities.'

'And how much did Agnes leave with him?'

'Slightly over a thousand pounds.'

Edward gave a low whistle. 'No wonder she required safe storage, since very few in Nottingham could lay claim to such a sum. I presume that she had a suitable receipt for the gold?'

'Of course, since she was somewhat astute herself in matters of business. That is why she looked so askance at her son's profligate habits. He is a popular figure in some of the more upmarket brothels and can regularly be found surrounded by fellow carousers in the White Lion, only a few doors from the house and workshop, and where he regularly loses considerable sums betting on cock-fights. Agnes was fearful that her late husband's fortune would rapidly disappear in such low pursuits and sought a way in which to keep it out of Thomas's hands. This is why, on the advice of her lawyer Giles Rattenbury, she drew up the loan agreement with me.'

'She loaned you the entire one thousand pounds?'

'Yes, but only on paper. The lawyer advised that if it were loaned to me, so that it remained in Greenwood's vault under my direction and control, then Thomas would cease importuning his mother for advances to be made to him against the inheritance that would eventually be his anyway. So the term of the loan was for the remainder of Agnes's life, to be repayable in full upon her death.'

'Therein may lie your salvation, Francis!' Edward enthused. 'Why would you wish Agnes dead? Quite apart from your affection for each other, were she to die you would be obliged to repay the loan.'

'In truth, I never touched a penny of it,' Francis assured him. 'That was not our arrangement — it was a mere fiction, and no doubt the entire sum remains untouched in Greenwood's vault.'

'Which is again to your advantage, Francis. But think upon something else — now that Agnes is dead, Thomas has access to the entire inheritance. He stood to gain much by her death, did he not?'

Francis's face took on a doubtful expression. 'I cannot think that he would be disposed to kill his own mother. He is a dissolute character in many ways, but I always gained the impression that he had much affection for her.'

'Or he pretended to,' Edward suggested. 'After all, if — as you advise me — he was constantly seeking money from her, it would have been in his best interests to maintain at least the pretence of affection, would it not?'

'You clearly suspect him of the deed,' Francis concluded gloomily, 'but what chance would I have of persuading a jury that a man would have recourse to slaughtering his own mother in so brutal a fashion?'

'You must leave it to me to secure the necessary proof of that,' Edward reminded him, 'although I shall need to visit you regularly for any further information you can supply me with.'

'I believe I have said all that I can,' Francis told him.

'Not quite everything,' Edward replied. 'If it be not too distressing for you to recall, you put me in mind of something else when you made reference to the brutal way in which Agnes died. I need you to tell me how your own person came to be so covered in her blood.'

Francis blanched as he recalled the scene that had confronted him when he awoke. 'I have assumed that, since I was lying next to her when she was so viciously hacked, some of the blood must have spurted over me as I slept. I cannot understand how I can have failed not to become aware of what was taking place only inches from me and why I was not myself murdered where I lay, but that was what must have happened. The chamber was dimly lit, since only a little of the late afternoon sun was filtering through the shutters and it was not until I reached for my hose that I noticed that they were covered in blood. I must have cast them off as we disrobed, for they were lying towards the foot of the bedding. All of this inclined me to the view that I must have committed the awful deed in my sleep and that I had somehow become bereft of my senses. Once they found my sword, with blood all over the tip of it, I inclined further towards that dreadful conclusion regarding what had transpired.'

'If you were so blood-covered yourself, did it not occur to anyone that you also had been attacked, but had survived?'

'That was the first opinion of the physician who was called in while others held me secure in the bedchamber. It was the man Morton who resides in nearby Swine Green. But he soon established that I had no wounds upon me and it was then that the constables arrived. I leave you to imagine the shame and humiliation I suffered, being taken in charge by men to whom I was accustomed to giving orders on a daily basis.'

'At least one of whom still has cause to be grateful for past kindnesses,' Edward said. 'It is thanks to Master Possett that I am able to visit you. You might seek to reward him — or at least thank him — once you are free of here.'

'If I ever am,' Francis replied morosely. 'If nothing else, your visit has encouraged me to believe that I was not the one who killed Agnes, but that will be of little comfort if I am to hang for it anyway.'

'You will not hang if there is anything within my power to prevent it,' Edward reassured him. 'So remain of good cheer and I will visit you again soon.'

'You are indeed a great friend and comfort, Edward,' Francis replied as tears rolled down his face.

Supper was almost over by the time that Edward returned home. Elizabeth sat frosty-faced in front of a half-eaten plate of cold meats, swilling down her second mug of strong beer.

'I thought to start without you,' she muttered, 'since I knew not when you would be returning, and the meats were beginning to curl at the edges.'

'I was visiting poor Francis,' Edward told her. 'He's very despondent and I can't say that I blame him. I've promised not to leave a stone unturned until I reach the truth.'

'Margaret has another tooth showing,' Elizabeth said, softening. 'You may remember her — she's your daughter.'

'I realise that you're expecting an apology,' Edward replied coldly, 'but I shall make no apology for attempting to preserve an old friend from the gallows.'

'I'm not the one to whom your apologies are due,' Elizabeth commented on her way out of the room. 'At the top of that list will be my parents, who've only seen their granddaughter three times during her first year of life.'

Edward sighed heavily. 'You are well aware that a journey to Ashby is quite out of the question at present. I'm fulfilling the duties of two bailiffs, while trying to save the life of one of them.'

Elizabeth turned before she mounted the first step. 'I prefer to call it the correct alignment of priorities. Good night, Edward.'

He muttered under his breath, then decided against any attempt to eat what was left on the table. The meat was indeed curled and dry, and he opted instead for flat beer. Then a second, followed by a third.

He took the fourth upstairs with him, in the hope that Elizabeth was already asleep.

3

Edward woke in a cold sweat the following morning, after a disturbed sleep in which he had dreamed of Francis struggling to remain afloat as he was dragged down the fast-flowing Trent, in peril of drowning. In his dream Edward had been on the riverbank, desperately holding out a hand to pull Francis from the churning torrent, but each time their hands touched Francis slipped from his grasp and was carried further downstream, with Edward racing along the bank in a fevered attempt to keep up with him.

Edward heaved a sigh of relief that it had only been a dream, then he remembered that the peril Francis actually faced was just as serious, and that he — Edward — was his only hope of salvation. He blinked in order to clear his sleep-glued eyes and reminded himself of the facts of the case.

Agnes had been hacked to death where she lay alongside Francis, who had been so insensible as not to be aware of what was happening so close to him. Agnes's blood had soaked both Francis and his hose where they lay near the foot of the bed. So far as could be determined, they had been alone in the house, and the three doors to the house had been locked from the inside.

First there was the main front door. Francis had told him that Agnes's son Thomas had keys to all the doors in the house. Edward would need to enquire as to whether or not anyone else either had keys, or had access to them. Where, for example, did Agnes keep hers, and had any of the servants been supplied with any? If it came to that, how many servants did the household possess? Surely a lady of Agnes's wealth would have kept a sizeable household, any one of whom could either have been entrusted with a key, or had an opportunity to have a copy made.

Then there was the rear door that led into the garden where, in common with all substantial houses in the town, the kitchen was located, safely away from the main house in case of fire. It was not uncommon for kitchens to have rooms attached to them for the accommodation of servants such as cooks, footmen and coachmen. The jakes was out at the back too, and this had been Francis's intended destination when he first awoke, only to find Agnes lying in her own welter.

Edward grimaced at the mental picture and hurriedly reminded himself that according to Francis the garden door had been locked on the inside by Agnes when she dismissed Mary.

Finally, there was the door that gave access between the house and the workshop where Thomas Timberlake continued the family business. Agnes had locked this communicating door from the house side, and had made a point of leaving the key in the lock. Clearly she did not want Thomas to enter the house while she and Francis were engaged upstairs, and Edward set to wondering how much, if anything, Thomas knew about his mother's relationship with Francis. How well did Thomas know Francis, and did he disapprove of Francis's presence in their lives? This was something Edward would need to check with Francis on his next visit to the cells underneath the Guildhall.

Edward would need to examine that door closely. If its foot was only a mere inch from the ground, he knew it would be possible to access the key that Agnes had left in the lock by the simple process of pushing a piece of thin parchment underneath where the key sat in its hole, then carefully inserting a thin object into the keyhole from the other side so that the key dropped out of the lock and onto the parchment, which could then be pulled under the door and through to the other side. Edward had known more than one burglar employ this ruse in order to pillage a house whose owners were sleeping in the false belief that they were safe from intruders.

If Francis had not committed the attack on Agnes — and Edward would not for one moment allow himself to contemplate that possibility — then someone had gained entry to the house while the two of them slept, and it had to be through one of those three doors. Then there was the matter of why they had both fallen asleep when they had obviously intended to engage in fornication. Edward had been married for long enough to know that the urge — particularly after a sufficient period of abstinence — heightened the senses and drove all other thoughts from one's head. Why, then, had they fallen asleep when they should have been tingling in every nerve? More to the point, *how* had that state come about? Had they been drugged? And if so, by what means, and by whose hand?

In the cot at the side of the bed Margaret snuffled and whimpered, in a sign that she would shortly be awake and bawling for something to eat. Edward slipped from under the covers and hurriedly climbed into his hose and tunic before she could awaken Elizabeth. Then he lifted his daughter from the cot and carried her carefully down the wooden stairs, hoping that its creaks wouldn't disturb his sleeping wife. As he reached the main room to the house he heard the muffled sounds of furtive activity from the scullery, and walked through with a smile at the sight of their maidservant Meg stirring the potage that she'd just brought in from the kitchen in the rear garden.

'Is any of that cool enough for Margaret?' he asked.

Meg nodded. 'If you take her to the table I'll bring it in for you.'

Ten minutes later the potage bowl was empty and there was a dirty spoon remaining to corroborate Edward's claim to have fed their daughter when Elizabeth appeared at the foot of the stairs. Wrapped in a floor-length robe over her nightdress, she smiled at the sight of Margaret snuggled into her father's chest, as he cooed and bounced her up and down on his knee.

'If you keep doing that, she'll spew up her breakfast,' Elizabeth told him. 'Here, let me take her while you clean the potage from your tunic.'

'She seems to want to spit out more than she consumes,' Edward observed.

Elizabeth nodded. 'I find it best to tease her first, by offering the spoon and then withdrawing it. This makes her more determined to eat what's on it. Still, it's a wonderful start to the day, to find my two most favourite people waiting for me downstairs.'

'I'm sorry I don't do it more often,' Edward replied softly and Elizabeth weakened for long enough to kiss him as he handed Margaret over.

'Please ignore what I said last night,' she said. 'I was tired, and I had a sore head which seems to have flown off overnight.'

'You were correct, though,' Edward admitted. 'I don't spend half as much time with the two of you as I should, and your parents could be forgiven for believing that we'd all died. I promise that when all this is over we'll ride down to Ashby to see them, but I couldn't begin to contemplate doing so now, while Francis is in peril of hanging.'

Elizabeth's parents lived half a day's ride to the south, where they occupied a grace-and-favour cottage as a reward for their many years serving the Zouche estate as steward and housekeeper. Edward and Elizabeth had married in haste after Sir Francis Willoughby had grudgingly offered no objection, and Edward hadn't met the pleasant old couple until months after their daughter became Mistress Mountsorrel.

The birth of their first child had presented another obstacle to travel, and even when he was only discharging his own duties, and not those of two bailiffs, Edward experienced the greatest difficulty in identifying a period of several days in which he could abandon the county to its own worst devices while he accompanied his wife and daughter to Ashby, so that the grandparents could fuss over their new addition to the family.

'Could you make this morning even more perfect by remaining to share breakfast with me for once?' Elizabeth asked.

'I might even be persuaded to return to bed afterwards,' Edward said with a wink.

She tapped his nose playfully. 'I was only offering breakfast. I know from experience that when you have a matter between your teeth like a hound with a rat, then your heart is not fully into our relationship, and I am not prepared to be a passing vessel on your river of priorities.'

'You should have chosen the life of a poet,' Edward said with a smile.

She grinned back at him. 'I will ignore the shallow flattery, which will no more get me back upstairs than any other ploy. So how go your enquiries on Francis's behalf?'

Edward's face fell as he told her that he had a long line of enquiries to make that he had not even started. 'Then there are those burglaries to the north of town, which Willoughby seems to think I should have resolved by now. I must give them more attention before he contemplates dismissing me.'

Just over an hour later Edward was seated in his temporary office in the Shire Hall, behind a desk that he did not officially own, and in a location that was entirely unknown to his employer. Sir Francis Willoughby, with his customary self-importance, had insisted that Edward base himself inside Wollaton Hall, Willoughby's grand mansion to the west of the town, completed five years previously, and with a magnificent deer park set in enough grounds to locate a town of its own. But the only good memories that Edward had of Wollaton centred around his surreptitious courtship of Elizabeth out of sight of her employer, and he wasn't about to ride for an hour in each direction between home and work.

He had therefore based himself in the Shire Hall, the law building that supplied the county with its own premises inside the town. For one thing, most of the crime committed in the county sooner or later proved to have links with the town anyway, and for another, while Edward was seated in the Shire Hall he was invisible to Willoughby out at Wollaton. He had no doubt that this arrangement suited Willoughby as much as it did Edward, even though Sir Francis would never lower himself to admit it. Provided that his bailiff presented himself once a week inside the morning room at his mansion in order to report progress, or lack of it, then no questions were likely to be asked.

Not that Edward was shirking his duties on behalf of the county — quite the contrary. It was simply the case that he preferred to conduct his enquiries without the pompous old fool breathing down his neck the entire time, and this morning was a perfect example of the wisdom of keeping one's distance from the fount of all ill-tempered demands for swift conclusions to outstanding matters.

Spread out in front of Edward on his battered desktop were the badly penned, and even more badly expressed, reports completed by his constables regarding the burglary complaints that Edward was supposed to be investigating.

They all involved the wealthier houses to be found in the outlying villages in the county. The country parson Martin Belfrage in Arnold, surgeon and bone-setter Alfred Denning in Basford, hosiery employer Nathaniel Braithwaite in Hucknall and farmer Jacob Astwell in Bulwell, plus half a dozen others, had, in recent weeks, reported that while they had been sleeping their houses had been pillaged by thieves who appeared to know what they were about.

These were not the usual run-of-the-mill outrages involving broken windows and forced door locks, followed by the hasty theft of anything that looked valuable or readily saleable. These men — and it had to be assumed that they were men, since Edward had yet to encounter a female burglar — were more sophisticated, both in their methods of entry and in the items that they stole. Entire windows and doors had been silently and painstakingly removed in order to facilitate the removal of paintings, statues, furnishings and tapestries from inside the premises, the sheer size and weight of which rendered it inevitable that more than one person had been involved, and that a coach or wagon had been employed to carry the items away.

Yet on not a single occasion had any of the householders heard so much as a cough or a whisper. These night-callers were experienced, and successful, and too intelligent to attempt to sell their ill-gotten goods locally. This was how burglars and other thieves were most commonly caught, by attempting to offload their haul on some town dealer who either peached on them in order to remain on friendly and unenquiring terms with the local constables, or were fool enough to offer them for resale on a market stall or in a shop window. The current possessors of these recently purloined items were almost certainly in an adjoining county, or perhaps even as far away as London, where the markets were larger and more wealthy.

Edward sighed and pushed the pile of parchments to one side. He'd make every effort to locate the stolen property, but he wasn't hopeful of any immediate success. He'd just have to hope that when someone lower down the chain of dishonesty — a village blacksmith, perhaps, who'd been called upon to sharpen an unusual tool — was in urgent need of a bargaining counter in exchange for not being run in for public drunkenness, they'd offer information that would lead back to those controlling the operation. If Edward's instinct was correct, and all these burglaries were the work of the same sophisticated team, then the entire parcel of rogues would fall like skittles hit with a well-aimed ball.

In the meantime, Edward had a friend in need and he could console his conscience with the thought that murder was a far more important matter than burglary. Duty, as well as friendship, dictated that he lost no time in speaking to those who might provide a clue as to who had actually killed Agnes Timberlake, and why. And he might as well begin with someone who had no motive to lie.

Physician James Morton smiled in vague recognition as he opened the front door to his spacious house in Swine Green in answer to Edward's knock. He looked the caller up and down with a seasoned professional eye and asked, 'Since you would appear to be in a disgraceful state of health, for whom are my services required?'

'For me,' Edward replied, 'but not because of any ailment of mine. You may recall that I was one of two law officers who called upon your talents some time ago, when we discovered the body of an unfortunate young woman in the premises of one Lavinia Temple in Newark Lane.'

Morton nodded. 'As I recall, she'd been strangled, then her body hung from a beam.'

'You are gifted with a sharp memory,' Edward flattered him, 'and I was hoping that you might have an equally clear memory of a more recent matter. The murder of the widow Agnes Timberlake in her home in Cow Lane?'

'I could hardly forget, given the amount of blood,' muttered Morton. 'Do please step inside.'

Edward declined the physician's offer of anything stronger than small beer, for which he was more than ready after the dusty ride to the north of the town.

'So what is it that you need to know?' Morton asked.

'I am currently undertaking, on a temporary basis, the duties of town bailiff on account of the fact that he who still holds that office is currently awaiting trial for the murder into which I am enquiring.'

'What need is there of further enquiry?' Morton asked. 'The jury found a true bill, did they not?'

'They did indeed,' Edward confirmed, 'but that does not of itself guarantee that there will be a conviction.'

Morton's eyes narrowed. 'As well as a colleague, this man is your friend, no doubt? Is your real purpose in calling here today to seek such evidence as will prevent his hanging?'

'Your perception is as acute as your memory,' Edward replied. 'But I simply ask of you that you recall such as you are able regarding what you found when called to the body.'

'I well remember the blood, at all events,' Morton began. 'It was everywhere, including all over the bed and along the floor. That was due in no small measure to the number of times that the poor woman had been hacked. I became familiar with battle wounds many years ago, when serving in Ireland under Sir Richard Bingham, and I can tell you without reservation that rarely have I seen so many fatal blows inflicted on one corpse.'

'Would the nature of such an attack have been such as to spray the immediate area with the lady's blood?'

'Did I not say so earlier? The man in the room with her — who I believe is your friend — had so much blood about him that I thought at first that he too had been attacked, although had that been the case it was surprising that he was still standing. In the event, it transpired that the blood was all hers.'

'And his sword is believed to have been the murder weapon?'

'Not by me, it isn't.'

'But surely…' Edward began, then stopped abruptly when Morton raised his hand.

'It is true that the man's sword was found in the same room. It is also true that there was blood on its tip, and given that no-one else was injured, I had to concede that it came from the corpse. But I could have told the constables, if asked, that the wounds inflicted on the unfortunate woman — at least, the ones that proved fatal — were probably not from that sword.'

'You were never asked?' Edward asked, aghast.

Morton shook his head. 'Those bone-headed constables simply asked me if the woman was dead — although they hardly needed a physician to assure them of that — and I heard the man admit that the sword was his, but no-one asked me to put the two facts together, and I was not being employed to investigate crime, merely to certify life extinct.'

'So what *did* kill her?'

Morton shook his head. 'I have not the remotest idea, and I remind you that my professional function is a limited one in matters such as these. I can only tell you that the weapon employed had a much broader, wider, surface than the tip of a sword, which was the only part of the blade with any blood on it. It would have been a more robust weapon, perhaps an axe, or a broadsword — one with a sturdier blade anyway. A sword wound tends to be thin and penetrating, whereas these wounds were broader. Still fatal enough, of course, but altogether much cruder. Finally, had the sword been the weapon used, I would have expected to see much more blood along it, most particularly the hilt, which was clean.'

'Would you be prepared to attend the assize trial and say the same thing?' Edward asked.

The physician nodded. 'Why would I not, since it's the truth?'

Edward smiled as he stepped back out into Swine Green. It was the first chink of light in the case. Now it was time to visit the house where Agnes was murdered.

4

The front door to the house in Cow Lane was locked, so Edward walked down the alleyway to the side, as invited by the sign that encouraged potential patrons to enter the workshop and admire 'the finest alabaster available, worked by master craftsmen'. There was no obvious sign of any master craftsman as Edward ducked under the lintel. The workshop was gloomy and appeared to contain only one person, a sallow-looking youth who was bent over a block of gypsum with a hammer and blade that he was employing in order to reduce the block to a smaller size.

The youth seemed to sense a presence behind him, and turned to face Edward. 'The master's gone 'ome for his dinner, but if you're 'ere from St Peter's Church, 'e said to tell you that your Saint Anthony will be ready by next Monday at the latest.'

'I'm no clergyman,' Edward said. 'I'm Edward Mountsorrel, and I'm fulfilling the role of town bailiff at present.'

'Because the other one's goin' to be 'ung, you mean?'

'Because the other one is currently awaiting trial,' Edward replied coldly. 'Now that you know who I am, who might you be?'

'I'm Ralph Meadows, the apprentice. What can I do for you?'

'Were you here on the day that the Widow Timberlake died?'

'The day she was murdered, you mean? Yeah, I was.'

'In this workshop?'

'Where else would I 'ave been?'

'In the house, perhaps. Don't apprentices get fed by their masters?'

'Yeah, they does, and this one gets fed with the master's family, down in Linby Lane. When 'e remembers, that is.'

'So you weren't in the house that day?'

'Not until all the fuss started, then the master told me to close the workshop an' 'elp the neighbours break the door down, then carry the body out. It were 'orrible.'

'Before that, you were here in the workshop?'

'That's right. The master come back from dinner — one of the days when 'e forgot to take me with 'im — and said he 'ad to meet someone in the town, so that left me to show a couple of customers the stuff we have on permanent display. Carved angels, birds, statues of saints, that sort of stuff. I was told to make a special point of showin' off the big statue of the queen that we've got out in the lane there — you must 'ave passed it on your way in.'

Edward was rapidly losing the thread of what the lad was trying to tell him, but two salient facts had already snagged his interest.

'So, on the afternoon that Mistress Timberlake died, you were here on your own, because your master had taken himself off somewhere. Then you had two potential customers who came into this workshop, and it was your job to try to interest them in what you had for sale, have I got that right?'

'Near enough. We always 'as a few samples on display, like I said.'

'So you were here with these two customers while your master was out at a meeting in the town?'

'Yeah, like I just told you. I came damned close to sellin' that statue of the queen that we've been trying to shift for a while, so I remember it well. In the end, the fellow said he'd think about it, but 'e never came back.'

Alarm bells rang in Edward's head. 'At one point you went into the alleyway there to show a customer the statue of the queen?'

'Yeah — do I 'ave to repeat everythin'?'

'Just one customer, or both of them?'

'Just the one — 'ave you been listenin' to me, or what?'

'Where was the other customer while you were out in the alleyway?'

'Back 'ere in the workshop, I suppose. He was interested in a grave ornament, and we keep all the samples of those here in the workshop.'

'And when did "all the fuss" start, as you put it earlier?'

'When I was still out in the alleyway with the customer.'

'Who was it who started this "fuss"?'

'That were the master. He must've come back from 'is meetin', because 'e was at the front of the 'ouse, yellin' about 'ow the door was locked and 'e'd left his key at 'ome.'

'Did he sound frightened, or apprehensive at all?'

'More annoyed, I'd say. But he *did* say something about it bein' funny that 'is mother wasn't openin' the door for 'im.'

'And what happened to your two customers when you and the neighbours started breaking the door down?'

'No idea, to be 'onest. Like I already told you, I was ordered to 'elp bring the body downstairs, and there were folk everywhere, shoutin' and carryin' on, so I couldn't tell you *where* they went.'

'Thank you for your assistance,' Edward said. 'I'll let you get back to your work.'

He turned to go, and Ralph Meadows went back to his laborious task. Edward heard the hard chink of hammer on metal, and turned back.

'That must be a hard job,' he commented casually.

Meadows turned to him again. 'You get used to the job after a while, when your 'ands get so calloused that you can't get blisters anymore.'

'What's that you're hammering into the stone?'

'It's not proper stone, only alabaster. As for the tool, it's called a "chisel". We use 'em all the time.'

Edward looked more closely at the tool, and his blood chilled as he formed a mental picture of it being driven hard into human flesh. 'It must be valuable.'

'Couldn't do this job without one,' Meadows assured him. 'They sometimes break, then we either 'ave to sharpen 'em, or use a new one.'

'So you have more than one here?'

'Three or four, usually. We keeps 'em in that pot in the corner there. If you're thinkin' of getting one for yourself, I could ask the master.'

'What would the county bailiff want a mason's chisel for?' came a querulous voice. A man was standing in a doorway that was presumably the one that connected with the house. Edward found himself staring into a set of cold grey eyes. 'And,' the man demanded, 'what is the county bailiff doing in my workshop?'

'Doing the work of the town bailiff, due to his unavoidable absence from duty,' Edward replied coolly as he locked eyes with the man.

'No doubt you'll be seeking a new town bailiff when that murderous bastard ends his days on Gallows Hill.'

'Before that can happen, there's the little matter of a trial,' Edward said.

The man's face set in a sneer. 'A mere formality. At least he's been given a little more time to make his peace with God than my poor mother was afforded.'

'I take it you are Thomas Timberlake?' Edward asked.

The man nodded curtly. 'Remind me of your name again, so that I know with whom to lodge my complaint?'

'Edward Mountsorrel, Bailiff to Sir Francis Willoughby, Sheriff of Nottinghamshire. As for lodging a complaint, you may find yourself at the end of a lengthy queue before Francis Barton comes to trial.'

'So you're sticking your nose in, no doubt in the hope of sliding your friend's head out of the noose that he so richly deserves?'

'I would like to think that those chosen to serve on his jury will do so with more of an open mind, Master Timberlake, which is why I'm making sure that they receive *all* the salient facts in the matter.'

'And what salient facts did you expect to get from my apprentice?' He turned to Ralph Meadows. 'Get back to your work, boy, instead of gawping at us.'

'Yes, Master,' Meadows muttered as he bent back over his allocated task.

'As a matter of fact,' Edward told Timberlake, 'I was hoping to speak with you, rather than your apprentice. But when I arrived here you were missing — not an unusual event, as I understand it.'

'I'm the master of my own business, and I keep such hours as I deem appropriate.'

'As you did on the day that your mother met with foul play,' Edward said. Timberlake's mouth set in a narrow line of distaste and he jerked his head back towards the dividing door.

'This is hardly a conversation to be conducted in the presence of a servant. Pray step inside.'

Edward did as invited, and Timberlake led the way into a rear ground floor room that was richly furnished as some sort of office chamber. He gestured for Edward to take a seat in one of the two ornate chairs while he lowered himself into the other.

'What did you mean by your reference to my absence on the day of my mother's murder?' Timberlake demanded.

'You were invited to supper, were you not?' Edward said. 'And there was to be another guest, Francis Barton, for whom your mother had a high regard?'

Timberlake snorted. 'That would be one way of putting it. He ensnared her with his physical charms, made a prostitute out of her, and thereby obtained the use of her legacy from my father.'

'You clearly have a low regard for the man,' Edward said.

Timberlake blundered on. 'He was a cheap adventurer on the make, and I have little doubt that when the truth emerges he will be found to have spent her entire fortune.'

'As he was entitled to do, given that the loan was for him to do with as he wished,' Edward pointed out.

Timberlake's eyes narrowed. 'Only for the duration of my mother's life,' he said. 'And now that she is dead we shall learn the truth.'

'The truth being what, exactly?' Edward asked.

Timberlake gave an unpleasant laugh. 'That there is nothing left, because the wastrel has squandered it all. That is why he murdered her, because she had learned the truth.'

It was Edward's turn to emit a hollow laugh. 'If what you allege is true, Master Timberlake, then the last thing Francis Barton desired was your mother's death, since the truth would then emerge when those who stood to inherit — presumably yourself — recalled the loan on the terms upon which it had been granted.'

'You are clearly not a man of the law, although you purport to uphold it in the name of the sheriff,' Timberlake sneered. 'These matters take time, and it will be months before Barton is held to an accounting of the money. Time he would not have had, were my mother to have revealed his treachery and called upon Master Greenwood to disclose how much of her inheritance remained within his vault.'

Edward sighed. 'It is yourself who lacks an understanding of the law, Master Timberlake. The money in question was freely available — in the form of gold, as I have been informed — for any purpose deemed appropriate by Master Barton. It would have been nothing untoward had he spent part, or even all, of it, provided that he accounted for it all upon your mother's death. So should there have been part of it missing when — and if — your mother sought an accounting of it, this would have been entirely within the terms of their agreement, would it not? Did you make enquiry of Mr Greenwood as to whether any of the gold had been removed from his vault, prior to making such wild allegations against Francis Barton?'

'I have not had dealings with Josiah Greenwood for several years,' Timberlake replied guardedly, 'since I have had no occasion to lodge money with him.'

'From which I may deduce that your business is not exactly thriving?' Edward asked pointedly.

Timberlake's cheeks flushed angrily. 'That is none of your business. But I *can* advise you the reason why Master Barton had been invited to join my mother and myself around the supper table on the day she died. It was in order that she might persuade him to allow me an advance on the inheritance that is destined to be mine anyway, with which I might expand my workshop.'

'You say that your mother was in favour of this advance being made?'

'So she assured me. She further advised me that Barton was resistant to the request, and that she suspected that there was nothing to be had in Greenwood's vault.'

'She said as much?' Edward asked in disbelief. 'Had she made enquiry of Master Greenwood?'

'I know not, but I had no reason to doubt what she said. I was therefore intending to confront Barton with her suspicion over the supper that, in the event, never took place.'

'A meeting which you were planning on attending covered in alabaster dust?' Edward asked quietly.

'Your meaning?' Timberlake bristled.

Edward was happy to oblige. 'You were promised an audience with the man who, according to you, held the key to money that you were seeking to persuade him to loan to you. While I am not myself a man of business, I would take the necessary steps to ensure that I was appropriately clad for such a meeting, and not dressed in dusty working clothes.'

'I had just returned from another meeting, and had not had time to change my garments.'

'Who was this other meeting with?'

'That is none of your business,' Timberlake replied, but Edward was not one to be lightly dismissed.

'But your attire explains why you did not have the key to your mother's front door about your person when you arrived for supper, does it not? I am correct in stating that it was necessary for you to call for assistance in breaking down the door when there was no answer to your knocking?'

'That is correct.'

'And the servant girl — Mary, is that her name?'

'Yes, what of her?'

'Where can I find her?'

'She has not been seen since that day, and no-one seems to know where she may be found. This is perhaps as well, since I shall have occasion to dismiss her anyway. My family will be moving into this house shortly, and we already have enough servants. In any case, I would not choose to employ one who runs from service at the slightest excuse.'

'Did it not occur to you that she might have been complicit in your mother's murder, and that this is the reason why she has gone to ground somewhere?'

'I know who was responsible for my mother's murder, Master Mountsorrel, and he is already securely in custody, awaiting his appointment with the hangman.'

'This girl Mary — what is her second name? And where does she live?'

'I have no idea, and even less interest in finding out.'

'Have you retained your mother's former servants?'

'Only Old George. He served in the Queen's Navy when they defeated the Spanish. My mother took pity on him when she found him begging in the Market Place, and gave him permission to abide in that rat-house behind the kitchen in exchange for feeding the pigs, emptying the jakes and suchlike. He's probably still around somewhere, although I shall lose no time in dismissing him once I move my family in. Now, are there any other questions you wish to ask? If not, then you will find the door in the same place that it was when you entered through it.'

Edward gritted his teeth to hold back a retort, and made his way back through the workshop, where the apprentice was still working away diligently at his block of gypsum. As he passed a workbench Edward caught sight of a large earthenware pot, inside which appeared to be several tools that resembled the one that Ralph Meadows was using, which he had called a 'chisel'. While Meadows' head was bent over his work Edward picked one of these implements from the pot and slipped it into his doublet pocket. Then, wishing the apprentice a cheery 'good day', he walked back down the alleyway that led to the street and ambled slowly past the front door to the house, looking intently for another side alley that must lead to the rear garden.

His initiative was rewarded several minutes later, as he found himself standing on an unkempt lawn that was badly in need of a scythe. To one side was a slightly listing structure that appeared to be the kitchen, and sitting in front of it was a man who, had he been located in the Market Place, could have been mistaken for a beggar. He looked at Edward with blank, disinterested eyes, and when there were only a few feet between them he asked, 'You've come to chuck me out, 'aven't you?'

'No, I haven't,' Edward reassured him. 'Are you by any chance Old George?'

'That's what they calls me, right enough,' the sad figure replied in a hoarse voice, 'but as far as I can reckon, I'm no more than thirty-five years old. But 'ow come you knows me name?'

'I came to thank you for the part you played in defeating the Armada, as did I in my own way,' Edward replied, evading the direct question and noting that one of the man's shirt sleeves was flapping emptily in the breeze, betraying the absence of an arm. George looked him up and down briefly before remarking, 'By the looks of you, you fared better than me.'

'I did indeed,' Edward confirmed. 'I was among the land troops under the Earl of Leicester, waiting at Tilbury for the invasion that never came, thanks to the bravery of men such as yourself, out there in the Channel.'

George smiled through cracked lips, happy to be able to recall former times when he possessed two arms. 'I were with Frobisher, on the *Triumph*. I were a gunner in them days, an' we 'arassed the Spanish from one end of the Channel to the other. Then we copped one amidships on the gun deck, and splinters went flyin' all over the place. I got one in me arm, but it were three days afore I saw the surgeon, because 'e 'ad more urgent cases — blokes what was dying and what 'ad lost their legs and such. By the time he got to me, the poison 'ad set in, and the arm 'ad to come off.'

'I don't suppose Her Majesty awarded you a pension for the loss of that arm?' Edward asked, and the man spat on the ground.

'Didn't even pay the wages I were due, any more than she did the rest've us. It took me three weeks to walk back 'ere, only to find that my wife didn't want a bloke what couldn't work, so I took to beggin', along with all the others. Then the Mistress found me and let me live 'ere in return for doing what jobs I could around the place. Ever tried digging gong out of an 'ole in the ground with only one arm?'

The question didn't seem to call for any reply, so Edward moved the conversation on.

'What about the other servants here — how did they treat you?'

'Kindly enough, 'specially Nell the cook. But Master Thomas told her that she weren't needed after the Mistress were murdered. None of us is, he reckons, so God knows what's going to 'appen to me. Back to the beggin', I suppose.'

This was hardly the time for Edward to advise him that the town constables under his temporary command included, among their many duties, the dispersal of beggars from public places. Instead he asked, 'What about Mary, the serving girl?'

George grunted. 'She didn't stay around here long enough to get 'er marchin' orders. Took 'erself back 'ome the day of the murder — leastways, that's where she said she were going. I 'ope she doesn't take to whoring, because she's a nice girl.'

'Let's hope not,' Edward agreed as he slipped a few pennies from his doublet and pressed them into George's hand. 'I'm afraid you probably *will* have to move on shortly, but here's something to help you on your way, in gratitude from one old soldier to another. I'd do the same for Mary if I knew where to find her. I don't even know her last name.'

'Thank you kindly,' George murmured. 'And if you mean it, then 'er name's "Blythe". Come from somewhere west o' the town, so far as I can remember. Lenton, maybe — or it could've been Beeston. Somewhere like that, anyroad.'

'Thank you, George,' Edward said softly. He reached down and touched the man's bony shoulder, before turning away with tears of rage in his eyes. All those brave men, reduced to the status of beggars in order to preserve the throne of an ungrateful queen who no doubt ate more for breakfast than George would eat in a week. No pension, no assistance, nothing. They'd outlived their usefulness, and could now rot in their own squalor.

Elizabeth caught the tortured look on his face as he walked back in ahead of supper.

'You must already have heard,' she commented, and when Edward raised two weary eyebrows in question, she explained.

'A messenger came from Sir Francis. He's been seeking you all day. You have until ten tomorrow morning to report to him at Wollaton Hall, or he'll be seeking a new bailiff.'

5

'This time there will be no prevarication, no excuses, and no disregard of my instructions!' Sir Francis Willoughby snapped as Edward stood, head bowed, in the morning room of Wollaton Hall. 'You will transfer your office to Wollaton with immediate effect, and that is a direct order! Are we fully *ad idem* on that point?'

'You overlook my additional duties in the town,' Edward mumbled.

'And *you* ignore your *primary* duties here in the county. You may set up your working space in the small room at the rear of the house, overlooking the Rose Walk. You may utilise one of the estate wagons to transfer papers up from wherever you've been hiding them in the town.'

'As you wish,' Edward mumbled. Then it occurred to him that something must have provoked this sudden storm. 'Was there something in particular that requires my urgent attention?' he asked.

Willoughby snorted. 'There are *several* matters, as it transpires. You have two more burglaries and a missing woman to investigate. Why is it that my messenger couldn't locate you either at home or in the Shire Hall?'

'I was out making enquiries,' Edward replied in justification, then braced himself for the riposte.

'Into the matter involving Bailiff Barton? Am I to assume that preserving your friend from the scaffold commands a higher priority than putting an end to the most outrageous burglaries that the county has ever experienced?'

'That depends upon how highly you value human life, sir, and whether or not it is thought to be important that the public retain any confidence in our criminal justice system.'

'The worthy folk of this county are almost certain to lose confidence in our justice system if we fail to apprehend this gang of thieves who are becoming increasingly brazen in their crimes.'

'Perhaps if you were to give me the details?'

Willoughby grunted and reached for a set of parchments on his desk. 'Here are the details, as reported to me. I require you to lose no time in riding out to each of these houses — one in Bramcote and the other in Chilwell — and commencing enquiries. You might also look in on this man Blythe and his wife in Wollaton village.'

'Blythe?' Edward echoed.

Willoughby nodded. 'Edmund Blythe and his wife, who live next to the church. Blythe is the supervisor at my coalmine. A valued worker, and a man worthy of encouragement. He wishes my assistance in finding his errant daughter.'

'*Mary* Blythe, by any chance?'

'How can I be expected to know her name? No doubt he can supply it, when you call on him and obtain further details about where she might be found. From what I could make out from the man's ramblings she had good reason to make herself scarce, but Blythe fears that she may have placed herself in some danger. Look into it without delay.'

'Before or after I journey to Bramcote and Chilwell, sir?'

'Devil take it, use your initiative, man! I'll tell Redmayne to expect you for a late dinner in the servants' pantry.'

This seemed as good a dismissal as any, so Edward bowed obsequiously and left the room, not muttering his first oath until he calculated that he was out of Willoughby's hearing. He opted to start his investigation at the furthest outpost and, mounting his horse, he rode out to the Chilwell house of Richard Holgate.

Edward dismounted outside the three-storey house and turned to admire the cathedral of glass that filled the field below it, inside which enormous tomato plants grew, their tendrils wrapped around a framework of wooden trellises.

'An experiment, merely,' came a soft voice from behind him, and Edward turned to find a grey-haired man in a fine blue doublet standing in the front doorway. 'But so far it has improved my tomato yield to such an extent that I am hopeful of being able to attempt the cultivation of oranges next year. The seed has already arrived from Spanish merchants, and the ground will be warm enough. But I suspect that you are not here in the spirit of horticultural experiment.'

'No, indeed,' Edward confirmed as he disclosed his identity. 'I am advised that you recently suffered a burglary.'

'I most certainly did,' Holgate grimaced. 'A most audacious one at that! The culprits used one of my own flat wagons to haul away my belongings. I can only hope that some of the fine porcelain items that I acquired during my travels in Southern France survived their rough journey into Beeston.'

'How do you know which direction they took?' Edward asked, intrigued.

Holgate smiled. 'The wagon they used had recently been in a crop field onto which considerable water had been poured, and as a result its wheels were covered in mud. On the whole the weather recently has been dry, and the marks left by the wagon expired somewhere along the road back east, near the Beeston Mill.'

Edward nodded and then enquired as to whether or not a list of stolen items had been compiled. He was invited inside to partake of a mug of beer while Mistress Holgate retrieved the list from her work desk in the front parlour.

'You neither heard nor saw anything?' Edward asked.

Holgate shook his head. 'I was awoken by my cook, Martha, who noticed that the front door was open when she came down in the morning to supervise the preparation of breakfast. When I say "open", that is something of an understatement — the door had been completely removed, in order to facilitate the carrying out of the cabinet that housed my collection of porcelain. It originated in Cathay, you know, and is extremely rare in England.'

'So not easily sold on, for example, in weekly markets?' Edward ventured.

Holgate burst out laughing. 'My good man, the collection was unique! Apart from its natural beauty, its true value would not be obvious to any casual buyer. There cannot be more than half a dozen men in England who might be interested in buying the pottery, and they would all be in London.'

Conscious that he had a busy day ahead of him, Edward took his leave of Holgate, assuring him that he would spare no effort in locating his somewhat unusual stolen property and those responsible for its theft.

A half hour ride north and he was on the outskirts of the village of Bramcote, where a sign pointed down a rutted lane towards Stapleford Hall, his next port of call. As he passed through an opening that led towards a very well appointed house, his path was blocked by two sturdy-looking ruffians armed with clubs. Edward advised them of both his identity and his authority, while reminding them that private armies were unlawful, and was led, by his horse's bridle, up to the grand house.

One of the men disappeared inside, only to re-emerge moments later with a portly middle-aged man who Edward surmised to be the proprietor of the imposing mansion, whose name Edward had been given as James Middleton. He bid Edward dismount, and voiced his apology.

'You must forgive my two servants here for their somewhat unwelcoming manner, but I have good cause to engage sturdy men to protect my property, after recent events that have necessitated their hiring.'

'If you refer to your burglary,' Edward replied, 'then that is why I am here.'

'You have caught the scurvy mumpers?'

'Not yet, but I am hopeful. Tell me as much as you can regarding what happened.'

'Come inside and sample some of my elderflower wine,' Middleton invited Edward. 'Though there is little I can tell you, since I was not here.'

Once the wine had been poured by an elderly steward, Edward complimented Middleton on its flavour.

His host smiled. 'I am a herbalist and apothecary by profession, so I am well placed to ensure that the produce of my hedgerows is put to good use. I own and preside over the apothecary located in Smithy Row, if you are familiar with the town. It is conveniently placed to the north of the Market Place, and has chambers above in which my family and I reside during the week, partly for our own convenience, but also in order that my two sons may attend the grammar school in Stoney Street. For that reason we are only here during the weekends, and then not always. One day I shall retire here a very wealthy man, God willing.'

'And this explains why you were not here when the hall was robbed?' Edward asked as he looked around the opulent chamber. 'I may say that they seem to have left you plenty, nevertheless. These chairs are of the finest.'

'What you see here are those items that were left,' Middleton said. 'It must have taken at least a small caravan of wagons to cart away what they stole in the way of furnishings, ornaments and wall hangings. But I do not mourn the loss of those items more than I weep for the deaths of my two dogs.'

'They killed your dogs?'

'They must have fed them poisoned meat in order to silence them,' Middleton told him as tears welled in his eyes. 'Two of the finest mastiffs I have ever known, bred from pedigree hounds on an estate in Derbyshire. They were called Brutus and Titus, and no-one dared set foot on my land unless they were properly leashed and under my command. They were allowed a free run of the grounds while we were absent in town. Even the house servants were terrified of them, and would only venture out when my groom had them secured to their chains.'

'So the thieves poisoned your dogs, then helped themselves to the contents of your house?' Edward concluded. When Middleton nodded, Edward asked, 'Did anyone in the house hear anything untoward?'

'All of them,' Middleton told him. 'But as they gathered to investigate what was going on, one of the group of five who were pillaging the contents of the house held them all inside the kitchen while brandishing a firearm.'

'Not your average burglars,' Edward commented, almost to himself. 'I shall need a list of everything stolen, and shall order that the county constables keep a close lookout for their appearance in unlikely places. Now, you may be able to assist me in another matter that pertains to your apothecary's wisdom.'

'You have an aching tooth?' Middleton asked solicitously. 'Or perhaps a blockage of the gut? A rash? The pox, even? I have simples for all these things.'

'It is not for myself,' Edward hastened to explain. 'Rather, it concerns another matter I am investigating. Is there some potion or draught that can be purchased easily, and whose effect is to launch those who consume it into a deep slumber?'

'There are several such,' Middleton nodded, 'but the best is perhaps valerian. It is a herb that grows here in the warmer counties of England and is easily extracted. It induces sleep in direct proportion to the quantity taken, but gives off a foul odour with a disagreeable taste, so is best consumed in a strong-flavoured liquid, such as wine.'

'And what are its effects?'

'That depends upon various factors. The quantity, obviously, but also the state of health of the person taking it. A strong and healthy man would need a moderate dose for natural sleep. In a standard wine mug, a two ounce sample would cause the average man to sleep for at least an hour, during which time you could strip him of his every garment and he would not be aware of what was happening.'

'And a woman?'

'If given the same dose, she would be insensible almost before she had put down the wine mug. She would then remain insensible for several hours. Regrettably, it is not unknown for a few wicked men to prey on unsuspecting young women in this manner.'

'So if, say, a jug of wine were consumed by a fit and active man in his middle years, and an older woman not given to vigorous exercise, they would both succumb but at different rates? And whereas the man might wake up within the hour, the woman could remain asleep for longer?'

'In general terms, yes,' Middleton confirmed. 'Although as I cautioned earlier, there are many factors that can have a bearing on how the dose takes effect.'

'And it is easily concealed within wine?'

'Wine would be the ideal agent of delivery, and is indeed the one I prescribe if one is to mask the smell and taste of the simple.'

'If the man were to awake afterwards, having consumed this dose, how might he feel?'

'He could well be confused as to his surroundings, and somewhat unsteady on his feet.' Middleton frowned. 'Do I deduce that such an event has occurred?'

'It has indeed, and I am most indebted to you, Master Middleton. But not half as indebted as a man currently confined in the Guildhall whose life you may have preserved, and who will be well placed to ensure that in future your town premises are more than adequately guarded. And so, if you would let me have that list of stolen items, I shall lose no further time in seeking them out, along with the miserable wretches who killed your dogs.'

Edward was almost singing as he guided the horse back over the hill that divided Bramcote from Wollaton and headed for the house of Edmund Blythe. He found it without difficulty, and tied his horse to a nearby tree before knocking on the door and waiting patiently for a response.

A slow shuffling could be heard from the other side of the door, then heavy breathing as the bolts were drawn back and the door creaked open. A lined and weather-beaten face fringed with grey hair peered out at him and demanded to know his business.

'My name is Edward Mountsorrel, and I'm the county bailiff,' Edward replied with an encouraging smile at the suspicious lady, who held the door open barely an inch. 'I come from Sheriff Willoughby,' he added, and the woman's face lit up in hope.

'You have news of our daughter?'

'None as yet,' he conceded, 'but with your assistance I intend to set about finding her.'

The woman opened the door fully and stepped back into the all-purpose room as she gestured for Edward to enter. She bid him take what appeared to be the only available seat, which he declined. 'I'll just sit on the floor here, if I may,' he suggested, and the woman nodded as she offered him scones and beer. In the belief that this was a modestly poor household he declined those also, and asked after her husband.

'Edmund's at work,' she told him, adding proudly, 'he's in charge at the coal diggings on the other side've the village. I'm Jane Blythe. Please, what do you need to know about our daughter?'

'Your daughter's name is Mary, Mistress Blythe?' Edward asked.

The woman nodded.

'And where did Mary work?'

'She worked in the house of a widow who treated her kindly enough; at least, that was until she came running back home.'

'And did she say why she was running back home?'

'Aye, she did, and it were nothing to be proud of, except she said she'd done it for love.'

'Done *what*, Mistress Blythe?'

Jane looked uncertain. Edward guessed that she was considering whether or not she should share a confidence, knowing that it may get her daughter into trouble, yet desperate to find her.

'The widow she worked for — Mary put something in her wine, but she never meant for her to get killed, honest she didn't! My Mary's not like that!'

Edward was somewhat taken aback at this sudden confession. 'This was in the house of the widow Agnes Timberlake, in Cow Lane, yes?' he enquired.

Jane had begun to sob. 'Mary told me that she placed some powder in her mistress's wine. She didn't know that the poor woman was going to be murdered! When she found out what had happened, Mary turned up here and told us all about it.'

Edward took a deep breath. 'That powder caused the widow and her guest to fall asleep, and while they were sleeping the lady was slaughtered in her bed, and the man with her was taken up for her murder. That man is my colleague and friend, Mistress Blythe, and I'll do everything I can to save his neck from the noose. But I must find Mary, and learn from her why she agreed to play a part in such a foul business. You said that she did it for love?'

Jane nodded. 'Mary's a right lovely lass, and the best daughter a mother could wish for, but she isn't exactly what you'd call comely. She was born with a birthmark on one cheek and takes after her father, rather large in the body, if you know what I mean. She never had boys chasing after her like the other girls in the village, and she took it to heart. I'm telling you this so you'll understand what happened next.'

'I think I can guess,' Edward replied. 'A man finally came along who showed some interest in your daughter. At his persuasion, she laced the wine with a sleeping draught while the widow was entertaining a gentleman friend.'

Jane looked pleadingly at Edward. 'She didn't know that they were going to murder the poor woman! Neither did the man she'd been walking out with — Owen, that's his name. They both thought that all that would happen was that the house would get burgled, but when it turned out that the lady had been murdered, they both ran for it. Mary turned up here to tell us they were both heading for Derbyshire, where Owen has family, so they could hide out until it was all over.' Jane wiped a tear from her face. 'When you find her, will she be taken in charge?'

'Probably,' Edward said. 'But I promise you that I'll be the one to take her in and I'll treat her gently. It may be that in return for what she can tell me she'll escape with a light punishment, if any at all. Do you have any idea where in Derbyshire they might have gone?'

'Not really,' Jane replied with a helpless expression. 'I think I caught a name like Mattock or Batlock, but I couldn't be sure. I was too busy trying to persuade her to stay, while my husband was taking a better look at this Owen fellow she was taking off with.'

'And what did your husband think of Owen?'

'He weren't all that keen on him, to tell you the truth. Said he was shifty looking, which is why we're worried about what might've happened to our Mary.'

'Leave it to me to find her, Mistress Blythe, and try not to worry unduly.'

She looked at him anxiously. 'Have you any children of your own, Master Mountsorrel?'

'Yes, a daughter, but she's barely a year old.'

'Well, you'll just have to hope that when she grows up she don't give you the worry that our Mary's given us.'

6

'Breakfast with my husband twice in the same week!' Elizabeth exclaimed as she came down the staircase with a sleepy Margaret in her arms. 'I must remember to withdraw bedchamber privileges more often.'

'I'm not here for long,' Edward said, helping himself to the fresh manchet loaf. 'I have much to do today.'

'How go your labours to save Francis from the hangman?' Elizabeth asked as she took the seat next to his and balanced Margaret on her knee.

Meg poked her head round the door from the scullery and confirmed that the potage was on its way.

Edward grinned at Meg then turned to his wife. 'Yesterday, I got the answer to one of the questions that had been troubling me; namely, how someone had gained entry to the house when the doors were all locked from the inside.'

'Clearly, someone from inside let them in, unless the intruder had a key of their own,' Elizabeth pointed out. 'Which was it?'

'The former — the servant girl let the murderers in while Agnes and Francis were in the upper chamber.'

Elizabeth nodded. 'And have you caught those burglars that Willoughby was complaining about?'

Edward shook his head. 'No, but once I get the right bit of information it shouldn't take long. The items they stole were quite unusual, and can't be easily disposed of.'

'Will you be needing more beer?' Meg asked, setting down the potage. 'If not, I'll set about the shopping, while the stalls still have fresh goods on them.'

Edward and Elizabeth shook their heads and Meg wandered back through the scullery to fetch her cloak and basket.

Edward watched her leave. 'We're very lucky to have Meg, after what I learned about the servant girl, Mary Blythe, employed by Agnes Timberlake. She's gone missing and I will need to ride to the adjoining county to look for her. I'm afraid that I will be away for a few days.'

'If you're going into Leicestershire,' Elizabeth replied, seizing her opportunity, 'then you could leave me at Ashby with my parents.'

'If I were, of course I would,' Edward said as he leaned across to ruffle the downy hair that adorned Margaret's head. 'But my search will take me west, into Derbyshire.'

'What do you know of Derbyshire?'

'Nothing, at present. But I shall call on its sheriff to assist me in seeking out Mary. And now I must be about my many tasks.'

'Will you grace us with your presence at supper?'

'I sincerely hope so. My final visit of the day will be with Francis.'

'Please give him my love and kind thoughts,' Elizabeth said.

'He might appreciate one of Meg's loaves more eagerly,' Edward replied as the thought struck him. 'Could you ask her to bake one and leave it for me to collect when I call back later this afternoon?'

'Only if you collect it from in here, rather than sneak into the kitchen behind my back. At least then I'll know that you're still alive.'

Edward rose, then leaned down to give her a parting kiss. 'The only danger I shall face today will be the tediousness of those to whom I need to speak in order to clear Francis's name of murder. Wish me well, as I go first to see a man about a loan.'

'It is customary for those who wish to engage my services to do so by first approaching my clerk,' the merchant Josiah Greenwood chided Edward in a thin, reedy voice as he contemplated him from down his nose.

Edward was far from discouraged. 'Then it is perhaps as well that I do not wish to engage your services, Master Greenwood. Instead I seek information from you regarding the loan of money by the late Agnes Timberlake to one Francis Barton.'

'What of it?' Greenwood replied sharply, his face set in a stern expression of resistance. 'Such matters are confidential, as you must be well aware, given your office.'

Edward sat facing Greenwood across his desk in the spacious building in Goose Gate. 'It is by virtue of my office that I am aware of the terms of that loan,' he reminded Greenwood tersely, 'and I do not need you to explain them to me. For that I would seek out the services of the lawyer who drew up the agreement, namely one Giles Rattenbury. My question to you is whether or not the amount lodged in your vault on account of Francis Barton remains untouched.'

'And my answer to you remains the same,' Greenwood replied coldly. 'These matters are confidential.'

Edward sighed. 'There are two ways in which the impasse could be resolved, Master Greenwood. The first is that I go to the trouble of visiting Master Barton, where he is currently languishing in one of his own cells, and obtain from him written permission to enquire into the current state of his holding. The second is that you simply tell me what I need to know by reference to your records — assuming that you keep any, that is.'

Greenwood bristled, as Edward had intended. 'I would not remain in business as the guardian of other people's wealth if I did not keep adequate records.'

'Then you should be well placed to advise me whether or not Master Barton has drawn any of that considerable sum in gold, believed to be worth around a thousand pounds.'

'And what makes you think that he may have done?'

'Not what, but *who*,' Edward corrected him. 'To be precise, Thomas Timberlake, who seems to be of the belief that Master Barton has spent most of that fortune and then murdered his mother Agnes when she discovered that fact. Although, as you yourself will agree, should Master Barton have wished to dip into that fortune, he was at liberty to do so, and need only have ensured that the full amount remained intact when the loan expired on Agnes's death.'

Greenwood sighed and rang a bell on his desk. The door to the chamber opened and an ink-stained clerk entered the room. 'Bring me the folio of the Timberlake lodgement,' Greenwood instructed.

The clerk bowed silently from the room, but omitted to close the door. A stiff breeze had been blowing along Goose Gate when Edward had hitched his horse to the rail outside and a sudden waft of air sent various parchments that had been lying on Greenwood's desk fluttering. Greenwood hastily held them down with his left arm while reaching urgently for an ornate vase with his right. Having secured the papers to the desk with the vase, he looked up impatiently as the clerk re-entered with the necessary folio.

'Master Biggins is here to see you,' the clerk told Greenwood, who grunted and took the folio.

Greenwood handed it across the desk to Edward. 'There you are — read it for yourself. The precise sum is one thousand, one hundred pounds and a few shillings. It has remained untouched since the day it was lodged in my vault.'

Edward cast his eyes over the documents. 'It would seem that Master Timberlake is over-anxious to cast the blame for his mother's murder on the one man who was acting in her best interests.'

'No doubt because that man was preserving her fortune from Thomas's own gambling debts.'

'Thomas sought an advance on his inheritance in order to acquire gypsum at a bargain price,' Edward corrected him.

Greenwood let out an unpleasant guffaw. 'Is that what the idle young sorner told you? It was only some weeks ago that he was seated where you are now, pleading with me for the loan of thirty pounds that he owed for wagering on the wrong game fowl in the White Lion. I sent him packing, but if you find him lying dead in some alley in the lower town, you might look to Daniel Gabriel for an explanation, since it is to him that Timberlake owes the money, and his terms of business are somewhat unforgiving.'

Edward stared at Greenwood. 'Master Timberlake assured me that he had not had dealings with you for several years.'

Greenwood shrugged. 'In a strict sense he hasn't, since I refused to do business with him. But if by that he meant that he had not met with me, then that was an outright lie.'

'Thank you for your assistance,' Edward said as he rose to leave. He now had confirmation that Thomas had a motive for the murder of his mother. Yet something else sat uncomfortably in his mind, like a stone wedged stubbornly in a horse's hoof. Something about Greenwood's chamber... Edward frowned; right now he needed to make his next call.

Physician James Morton opened his front door with a smile that faded instantly when he recognised the caller. 'I was hoping that you were a patient with an ailment,' he grumbled, 'but come inside anyway.'

'No need,' Edward replied as he extracted the chisel from his doublet, 'provided that you can confirm that this — or something of a like nature — could have been used to kill Agnes Timberlake.'

Morton took the chisel from Edward's outstretched hand and examined it through fading eyes, then nodded. 'It was certainly more likely to have been the cause of those appalling injuries than that sword of your friend's,' he observed. 'Where did you get it?'

'That's for me to know, and you to speculate upon,' Edward said with a grin, as he made his way with even greater confidence to the place from where he'd stolen the item in question.

Thomas Timberlake gave Edward a venomous stare as he walked into the workshop. 'What do you want this time?' he snarled.

'An explanation as to why you lied to me about not having had any recent dealings with Josiah Greenwood, when in fact you were at his premises in Goose Gate in recent weeks, seeking a loan to cover your gaming debts.'

Timberlake gave a sharp hiss and indicated with a flick of his head that he and Edward should step into the side alley. 'Who told you about that?' Timberlake demanded. 'And keep your voice soft, since it is not a matter suitable for the ears of an apprentice.'

'Greenwood himself told me, less than an hour ago,' Edward said. 'So I repeat my question — why did you lie to me?'

'I was embarrassed by the fact that I owed money to one of the town's most infamous usurers,' Thomas muttered, his eyes on the ground. 'But I did not go to Greenwood — it was he who summoned me and offered to loan me the money at even more outrageous rates than Gabriel. I declined, and we parted on bad terms, and by the time that I got back here in anticipation of supper my mother had been slaughtered.'

'So let me see if I have this right,' said Edward. 'Your meeting in town on the day of your mother's murder was with Greenwood? And it was at Greenwood's behest?'

'Did I not just say so?'

'My thanks for your candour — at last,' Edward said as he turned to leave. He glanced up at the windblown clouds, through which a watery sun appeared to be hovering over Nottingham castle. It was now mid afternoon, but so far his day had been very rewarding, and he would be home in ample time for supper.

Francis looked up eagerly as Edward was admitted to the cell in the Guildhall. The pungent smell was no better, a mixture of unwashed skin, dank walls and a full slop bucket, but Francis's mood appeared to have lightened as Edward handed over the freshly baked loaf that he had collected on his brief return home.

'I've remembered more of what happened, and it may be important!' Francis said as he shook Edward's hand then sat back down on the straw palliasse.

'Tell me while you remember, then I shall impart some good news of my own,' Edward replied.

'It was as we were heading for the bedchamber after having partaken of some wine,' Francis recalled. 'Agnes was complaining that she felt unsteady on her feet, and as she stooped to remove her slippers she lost her balance and fell onto the bolster. She giggled and invited me to undress her, which took longer than it might otherwise have done because I myself was beginning to experience a certain dizziness. My last memory is of pulling the covers over her nakedness, then sliding in beside her and wondering if it would be ungallant of me to go to sleep. Were we drugged, think you?'

'Yes, most certainly. A powder was added to the wine served by the serving girl, Mary. It seems that she was prevailed upon to do that by a man with whom she had recently taken up, and that she then unlocked the door between the downstairs chambers and the adjoining workshop. She was of the belief that this was all in order that the house could be burgled, and had no prior knowledge, or desire, that Agnes was to be murdered.'

'You have spoken with her?' Francis asked, breathless with excitement. 'If she is prepared to tell the truth before a jury, then I shall be a free man once more!'

Edward shook his head with a frown. 'She ran away immediately after realising what she had been a party to. She called into her parents' home in Wollaton for long enough to pass on all the information I have just shared with you, then she took off with the man who had talked her into it. They were seemingly heading west into Derbyshire. I shall set out in search of her on the morrow.'

'So Agnes was killed by burglars?' Francis asked.

Edward shook his head again. 'I think not, since so far as we are aware nothing was stolen, although the house was richly endowed with furnishings and other valuables. I believe her death to have been connected with the fortune that she had lodged with Josiah Greenwood, and over which you had control.'

'That gives me a motive, does it not?'

'No, you would not have benefitted financially from Agnes's death unless you had embezzled all her money, which you assure me you have not. We must therefore look to someone else who stood to benefit from her death, and my enquiries have all but identified Thomas Timberlake. Upon his mother's death he would become the heir to her fortune, and I have discovered that he was in debt to the tune of thirty pounds to Daniel Gabriel.'

'God preserve him!' Francis muttered. 'Gabriel is known to collect unpaid debts by the pound, the pounds in question being in human flesh. We once found one of his victims by the Poor Hospital, where he had crawled with only one leg. He died before he could swear an oath as to the identity of his assailants, and no-one could be found to testify. The poor devil was fifty pounds in debt to Gabriel, according to our enquiries. If Thomas owes him money, then he will be desperate to repay it. But surely, his alabaster business could have covered the debt?'

'It seems to have fallen by the wayside recently, no doubt due to Thomas's fondness for gambling. But if he could demonstrate that he was about to come into a thousand pounds, perhaps even Gabriel could be prevailed upon to wait for repayment, albeit at a usurious rate. Thomas has admitted that he had in fact met with Josiah Greenwood on the afternoon that you were with Agnes, and was returning from there when he found the house locked against him. He may have lied to me about his reason for that meeting, but it seems to have been an attempt on his part to borrow the money to pay off Gabriel.'

'If only you can find Mary, we can perhaps learn more regarding who gained entry to the house and claimed my sword.'

'That's something else,' Edward said. 'I have evidence that the dreadful deed was done with a chisel, which is a metal tool employed in Timberlake's enterprise, and not with your sword. If we assume that whoever did the deed was waiting in the workshop for the door to be opened from inside the house, then he would have seen such a tool lying around and taken his opportunity.'

'Would this theft not have been noticed by those working in the workshop?'

'There is only one person employed by Thomas, and that is a young apprentice who does what he is told. On the afternoon of Agnes's murder his attention was engaged by two men posing as potential customers, who were no doubt there to distract the lad. While one of them lured him outside on the pretence of examining a statue that they had long been seeking to sell, the other one remained inside the workshop, and would therefore have been there when Mary unlocked the door.'

'You have performed wonders in such a short time,' Francis enthused, 'but I am told that an assize has been set for two weeks hence, so the sooner you find Mary, the sooner the truth may emerge.'

Edward reached out and gripped Francis by the shoulder. 'Do not build up your hopes too much, my dear friend. I hold out no great prospect in finding the girl, and even if I do, she may well be terrorised into silence. We must place our trust in God and the truth.'

Francis stood and pulled Edward into a hug. 'I would rather place my trust in Edward Mountsorrel. And please thank Elizabeth most profusely for this loaf. For the first time in a week I feel hungry enough to eat.'

7

The sun was high as Edward guided his horse along the stony track north of Derby that would lead him to Ashbourne, according to the marker stone. He had left behind the gently sloping fields of Nottinghamshire, their hedgerows bursting with wildflowers, and was now travelling through the undulating valleys and river courses of Derbyshire.

Edward drew some consolation from the fact that the sheriffdoms of Nottinghamshire and Derbyshire were no longer combined, as they had been until a quarter of a century earlier. If they had remained under one sheriff, then instead of the gentle wooded glades of the county of Nottinghamshire, with which he was now familiar, he would be attempting to enforce law and order in these remote valleys, with their gaunt outcrops of rocks, plunging streams and seemingly impossible tracks.

As the horse breasted yet another hill, Edward's thoughts returned to the task at hand. He feared that he may not be able to locate Mary Blythe, or, more ominously, that she may already had outlived her usefulness to the murderers hired to kill Agnes Timberlake. Edward's only hope was that perhaps 'Owen' had some other purpose for her, even if it was only the obvious carnal one.

If an assize jury was to be called upon to acquit Francis because someone else had been admitted to the house in order to commit the foul deed while Francis himself was unconscious, then either Mary herself would have to appear and tell the court what part she had played in the overall business, or her absence would need to be satisfactorily explained and her mother would need to tell the jury about her daughter's confession.

Up ahead Edward saw a church spire rising out of yet another deep ravine. He hoped that he was approaching Ashbourne, where the county sheriff, John Cockayne, resided. There had been a sharp exchange with Sir Francis Willoughby when Edward had announced his intention of taking a few days out of his duties to locate Mary. He had made the mistake of explaining that her evidence could be crucial to Francis's defence, when Willoughby seemed far more interested in identifying the thieves who were causing so much trouble in the wealthier houses of Nottinghamshire. Edward had been forced to remind him that Willoughby himself had tasked Edward with investigating Mary's disappearance, and that her father was an important worker in the coalmine that was the foundation stone of the Willoughby family's fortunes. Sir Francis had relented, to the extent of giving Edward the directions he was now following.

He'd spent the previous night at an inferior inn in a place called Osmaston, whose only advantage, so far as he could tell, was that it put him further along the road he needed to travel. At least it meant that it was barely past midday when he hitched his horse's bridle to the rail outside an imposing three-storey house in the centre of Ashbourne before making use of the door knocker. A servant came to the door and Edward advised him that he was on official business on behalf of the Sheriff of Nottinghamshire. He was shown into a large room at the front of the house and asked to wait while the servant fetched his master.

Sheriff Cockayne strode into the room and greeted Edward warmly before inviting him to state his business.

'I am seeking a young woman who has gone missing,' Edward explained. 'She was last seen in the company of a man of dubious character and she announced that she was intending to visit some place within your jurisdiction that has a name like "Mattock" or "Batlock", although I am sure that this is not quite its correct appellation.'

Cockayne crossed the room to study a map of the county that was displayed on the wall. Then he tapped his finger on it.

'I think you mean Matlock,' he said. 'It's a full day's ride north of here, and I'd be happy to lend you the services of the local constable once you get there. I'll supply you with a letter of reference. If you set off early tomorrow morning you should reach his cottage before sundown. I'd be honoured if you'd accept my hospitality for tonight.'

Edward was delighted to receive such an invitation and more than happy to relax around the supper table with the sheriff, along with his wife and two teenage children.

The next morning, after a most generous breakfast, he took the track to Matlock, passing through quaint villages with names like Kniveton, Bradbourne and Cromford. He made good progress and the sun had barely begun to sink to the west when he found himself knocking on a cottage door that, he had been told, was the residence of the local constable, Richard Grindley.

Grindley invited him in, insisted that he down several mugs of small beer to remove the dust of travel from his throat, and demanded that he help himself to some of the delightfully creamy local cheese, named apparently after a nearby valley called Dovedale.

'So, tell me, what brings you up here in the course of your duties?' Grindley asked. 'It must be something important, to bring you this far out of your way.'

'I'm looking for a young woman from Nottinghamshire who's gone missing in recent weeks,' Edward explained. 'She was last heard of in the company of a man calling himself "Owen". Her parents are most concerned for her welfare, and as coincidence would have it she could also be of great assistance in the investigation of the murder of her late mistress. Her name is Mary Blythe, although she may of course be using another name. She's a mature lass, in her twenties, and she's described as having a birthmark on one side of her face. Have you seen anyone like that around these parts recently?'

Grindley shook his head. 'I know everybody around these parts and I've never seen a lass answering that description. But we can ask around the local alehouses in case she and her companion have been seen in any of them, as well as the local farms, in case they've been seeking work of some sort. This is a small place and if they've been here recently we'll soon find out. I take it you won't want to start until tomorrow?'

'Probably not,' Edward confirmed. 'In which case, can you recommend an inn for me to engage for the duration of my stay?'

'That's easily fixed,' Grindley said with a grin. 'My brother and his wife run "The Crown", in the main street of the village, down the track there. In truth, The Crown's probably the only place where you can be sure of not being eaten alive by lice. I'll take you down there when you're ready.'

Later that evening, Edward contentedly tucked into a generous supper of salted fish, bread, lamb cuts and fruit that the affable landlord of The Crown placed on the table in front of him. His mug was regularly replenished with a locally brewed ale that had a rich, nutty taste, and he happily drank his fill.

His thoughts eventually turned towards making his way to the chamber upstairs in which he'd already deposited his few possessions, but the task suddenly seemed more difficult than he'd anticipated. As he stood up, the room in which he'd been supping slowly began to rotate before his eyes. Then it swung back the way it had come. Edward staggered and the floor suddenly lurched up towards him as he fell senseless across the table.

Edward slowly regained consciousness only to find himself lying in almost total darkness. His head pounded and his mouth was as dry as a sack of hay stubble from the gag stuffed into his mouth. He attempted to raise an arm to pull out the gag but realised his arms were tied securely behind his back. A brief attempt to rise from whatever he was lying on only served to confirm that his ankles were also tightly fastened to it, as well as being secured by rope to each other.

Edward took a deep breath and was just about to yell out, when he heard a door creak open, and stealthy footsteps creep towards him. He commended his soul to God, closed his eyes tightly together and awaited his fate.

8

Instead of cold metal hacking into warm flesh, Edward felt a gentle hand remove the gag from his mouth, and he opened his eyes in surprise.

'Don't make a noise, else they'll 'ear us and we'll both be dead,' the young woman warned him as she struggled with the ropes around his feet.

'Untie my hands first, then I can do the rest myself,' he whispered hoarsely, and she transferred her efforts to his wrists.

As Edward's hands were bound behind him, it wasn't until the young woman had worked her way through the knots that he finally got a good look at her face. A shaft of moonlight penetrated through the window casement and he could clearly see the livid red mark on the left-hand side of her face, from just below her eye to a point where it disappeared down her neck.

'Mary Blythe?' he whispered.

She nodded awkwardly. 'Yeah. You've been looking for me, and now you've found me. Or rather I've found you. I want to go back to Nottingham, and I need you to protect me from them.'

'Them?'

'I'll tell you later. Now, can you walk?'

Edward rose to his feet and gingerly walked up and down, trying not to cause any floorboards to creak as he did so. He looked at Mary. 'I've still got the use of my legs, it seems, so now what?'

'Out the window,' she told him with a nod. 'There's a plant growing up the wall that we can climb down and the roof of the stables is just below. Then we ride as hard as we can, and if anyone comes after us, you can kill them, right?'

'If I have to, yes,' Edward confirmed, before realising that he was unarmed.

'I don't suppose you brought my sword?' he asked.

'It's down in the stable, with your horse. I pinched it while they were all getting drunk. Now come *on*, before they notice that I'm missing.'

Edward peered over the window ledge and assessed the distance down to the roof of the stables. It appeared to be just over six feet — little more than his own height. If he was able to hang from the ledge and drop gently, it would probably not be necessary for him to cling to the vines that were growing up the wall, and looked to him unlikely to bear his weight. He looked back at Mary. 'You first, in case that greenery isn't as sturdy as it looks.'

She nodded. 'Good job I'm not wearing my skirts.'

He realised for the first time that Mary was dressed for horse riding, in what looked like a man's reinforced hose under a short bodice of some sort. The hose were tucked into a sturdy pair of boots and a riding cloak hung around her shoulders. As he watched, Mary swung herself over the ledge, then climbed deftly down the most sturdy stem of the vine until she landed soundlessly on the roof of the stables. Edward was impressed.

Now it was his turn. He slid over the window ledge, said a silent prayer, then let his full bodyweight hang down as his hands took the strain. Guessing that his feet were no more than a foot from the stables roof, he let go, and landed with a soft thump on his designated target. Mary had already lowered herself down from the roof and was waiting him by the stable door. He did the same, then crept to her side.

'I gave the stable boy some of the powder that they gave you,' she whispered. 'Same as I give the Widow Timberlake and her lover that day she was killed. Come on, let's get out of here.'

They led their horses out by their bridles, Edward having retrieved his sword from the hay to the side of his mount. Mary was about to leap into the saddle of her grey mare when Edward issued a low warning. 'No, we walk them out slowly and quietly until we're well down the road. Follow me!'

Ten minutes later they were on the moonlit track that led back to Ashbourne, and as they climbed into their saddles it was Mary's turn to issue a muted instruction. 'Not that way — follow me.'

Edward did as requested, and once they were a mile or so from the inn he felt able to employ his normal voice. 'Where does this road lead?'

'Home,' Mary replied. 'You must have come by way of Ashbourne, right?'

'Correct,' Edward confirmed. 'So why are we going this way?'

'It's a quicker way back to Wollaton,' she told him. 'And there's something you need to see down this road.'

A pale light had appeared to the east as they rode into a secluded valley just beyond a small hamlet called Tansley. Mary indicated a narrow track that led through a wood. As they emerged from the trees, Edward could see a large barn-like structure in the middle of a field. Some of the high grass had been flattened, indicating that wheeled vehicles had travelled across it fairly recently. They guided their horses into the overhang of trees and Mary nodded towards the building. 'If you look in there you'll find lots of stolen stuff.'

'Stolen from where?' Edward asked as a wild hope surfaced.

'All over the place, but mainly round Nottingham. It wasn't me that stole it, but Owen showed it to me when we came up here after the widow got murdered. If you're the Nottingham bailiff, like Owen reckoned, then you need to go inside, and you'll see that I'm not lying to you. Then you might let me off what I've done.'

'We can't go in now,' Edward cautioned her, 'since it'll soon be light and we have to get back to Nottingham. I can bring constables back here later. The most important thing at the moment is to keep you safe.'

Mary nodded in agreement. 'Nottingham is two day's ride from here, even taking this quicker road. We better get back on our way.'

'We can't risk travelling by day,' Edward said as he looked anxiously up at the rapidly lightening sky. 'We need to find somewhere to hide until it gets dark again, then we can get back on the road.'

The sun had fully risen when they finally spotted a large wooded area down a track a few miles south of a village whose milestone displayed the name 'Wessington'. They rode into the centre of the wood before tying their horses' bridles to suitably sturdy oak trees, then looked around until they found a hollow in the earth surrounded by bracken and other ground foliage. Edward announced that they would spend the day there and would not be venturing out until it was dark again.

'I met your mother,' Edward told Mary, once they had set up a rough camp. 'She and your father are very worried about you, and your father's employer gave me permission to come looking for you.'

Mary seemed relieved to hear that her parents hadn't disowned her.

'I had a reason of my own for looking for you,' Edward continued. 'I believe that you can provide information that will enable a good friend of mine to escape the noose for something he didn't do.'

'This friend — is he the fellow Widow Timberlake was entertaining?'

'That's him. His name is Francis Barton and he is — was — the town bailiff. I need you to tell the court that he couldn't have murdered Agnes Timberlake because you drugged their wine on the afternoon that the widow was murdered. Perhaps you might even be able to reveal who did.'

'Then they'll hang me, right?' Mary asked miserably.

'I won't let that happen,' Edward reassured her. 'Are you prepared to trust me?'

Mary nodded. 'What other choice do I have?'

'Why don't you tell me all about yourself, and how you came to be putting a powder in your mistress's wine?' Edward suggested.

He listened with a growing sympathy as Mary told him her story. She told him of her miserable childhood, when the other children in her village had cruelly made fun of her birthmark, even suggesting that it was the Devil's mark. Then, as she matured, the local boys began to show her plenty of attention of entirely the wrong sort, and she'd been sent by her parents to Nottingham to stay with her aunt, who'd lost no time in finding her a place as a scullery maid in a wealthy local household.

Mary had worked her way up until she was hired by Agnes Timberlake as a general domestic servant, in which capacity she'd found permanence of a sort, although she still dreamed of finding love and becoming a wife and mother, with a house of her own. Then she had met a man calling himself Owen Drinkwater.

He had approached her whilst she'd been out shopping at the produce market in Weekday Cross. After several meetings, she'd taken to visiting him once a week at a dwelling in Narrow Marsh, where he lived with a group of male acquaintances. Inevitably, Mary had fallen for Owen, believing she'd finally found the life partner she craved.

Edward was only too familiar with the stinking cesspit that was Narrow Marsh, through his occasional joint operations with Francis Barton, whose thankless task as town bailiff it had been to maintain some sort of law and order in what was in effect a rat-run for the lowest sorts of refugees from justice. If an arrest was to be effected in Narrow Marsh, several constables armed with heavy clubs were often required, and even then they could anticipate violent resistance from the resident thugs, pimps, cutthroats and robbers who made up the bulk of its population. Whoever Owen Drinkwater and his 'acquaintances' were, they would hardly be suitable company for a naive young woman.

Edward could guess the rest of Mary's story, but he let her tell it nevertheless.

After a few weeks, it dawned on Mary that the men with whom she was surrounded on her afternoons off were villains, who openly boasted of their burglary exploits in fancy houses to the north of the town. The fine furnishings, ornaments and other valuable items that they had stolen were being sold on by some shadowy character they referred to only as 'Himself'. Then came the invitation for her to join them and share in the spoils.

At first, Mary had been shocked and reluctant, particularly when told that their next target was to be the house in which she was employed. But when Owen assured her they could use the proceeds in order to set up a home together, she'd finally weakened.

On that fatal day, she'd slipped a quantity of a suspicious-looking powder into the wine jug that her mistress was sharing with her lover. Then, after she had been dismissed for the afternoon, she waited in the garden until it had all gone quiet in the house before letting herself back in through the rear door with her own spare key. As directed, she unlocked the adjoining door to the workshop and had then gone back to her own room behind the kitchen, to wait for Owen to confirm that the house had been stripped of everything worth taking.

She began to sob as she recounted how Owen had come to collect her in a hurry. He had told her that her mistress was dead and that she would be blamed for it unless she lost no time in running away with him. When she'd asked to be allowed to remain to protest her innocence, he'd dragged her to a waiting horse. They'd ridden fast towards the outskirts of town, stealing a second horse from outside an inn close by Chapel Bar, then riding hard to Wollaton.

'And then you came to Derbyshire?' Edward asked.

Mary nodded. 'Not that I had any choice. They were awful to me, and I was already planning how I was going to get away from them when you came along, and I saw my chance.'

'How did you learn about me?' Edward asked, although he thought he already knew the answer to that question.

'We were all at the inn where you were staying when the brother of the landlord came in and said that you were looking for me. I thought they were going to kill me at first, but then they decided that they needed to know what you knew about the burglaries and the murder of Widow Timberlake, and they forgot all about me, thank goodness.'

'They miscalculated badly there,' Edward said, 'since I knew nothing — not even where you were. And what I now know about the burglaries I got entirely from what you've just told me.'

'So you won't have me locked up and hung?'

'Of course not. The information you can give will not only save Francis Barton from the gallows, but will also lead to the capture of all those wrongdoers, and the recovery of much stolen property. Sheriff Willoughby will be delighted!'

'Will I be allowed to see my mother and father again before you take me to give evidence?'

'I can probably risk taking you back to see your parents, to let them know that you're still alive. But after that we'll need to make arrangements for you to stay somewhere safe until this gang can be taken into custody.'

'Do you know of somewhere?'

'I do, if you don't mind going back into domestic service for a while. I have a fine house in Nottingham, on Whitefriars Lane, and although we already have a house girl called Meg, the duties sometimes get a bit beyond her, so you could help out. There's a spare room next to Meg's, behind the kitchen. But I'm afraid you won't be allowed to leave the house or garden — it will be too dangerous if someone sees you.'

Mary nodded her agreement.

'How long do you think it will be before we reach your parents' home?' Edward asked.

Mary shrugged. 'Two more nights at least.'

'Once we're past Alfreton, if we were to drive the horses as hard as they can go, do you think we can make it to Wollaton after one more daytime stop?'

'I think so,' Mary replied.

As night began to fall they crept from their hiding place, untied the horses that had been happily grazing on the grass all around them, and together they cantered south. They reached Alfreton within the hour, and as one darkened village was followed by another the milestones on the roadside began to count down towards their ultimate destination. Dawn was on the horizon as they slowed the horses to a trot through Kimberley, where a signpost advised them that they had entered Nottinghamshire. Edward's spirits rose.

'Can't we just keep riding?' Mary asked.

'You wouldn't ask that if you were one of our horses,' he replied, 'and we don't want one of them to fall over when we're in sight of home. But if it makes you feel any happier, I will try and find us some food when we make our next stop.'

They had almost reached Nuthall when they passed a well-appointed inn on their left, ahead of which could be seen a large expanse of water surrounded by trees. Edward nodded towards it, and a short while later they had hitched both horses to the same stout oak and made their way to the water's edge. A boat had been hauled up onto a sandy foreshore and behind it was a somewhat dilapidated hut in which it was no doubt stored during less clement weather.

'Find somewhere comfortable in here to hide, while I go in search of food,' Edward instructed Mary. 'Don't show yourself outside.'

After what seemed like an eternity waiting in the rapidly warming sunshine, Edward was rewarded by the sight of a bread cart being pulled up the road by an elderly horse, with a young boy at the reins. Edward stepped out into the road and flagged him down, exchanging a sixpenny piece for an armful of bread that was still warm, and which would not now be available for purchase by the landlord of the inn. He took it back to a grateful Mary, who was already chewing her way into the third small loaf when she burped loudly and turned pale.

'Slow down,' Edward urged her. 'I don't want you coming down with a stomach ailment when we're only a day away from home.'

Mary was asleep barely an hour later, and Edward was obliged to rouse her as he saw the sun disappear below the horizon. She opened her eyes and smiled. 'We're still alive, and going home today!'

Edward nodded. 'Drink your fill from the lake outside and then we'll be on our way.'

They set the horses into a steady trot, and the miles fell away in the clouds of dust that their horses' hooves kicked up behind them. The sky was growing light to the east when Edward gave a shout and pointed ahead of them. 'Unless I'm much mistaken, you should recognise that church spire up ahead.'

Mary raised herself up out of the saddle, and gave a cry of her own. 'You're right! I never thought I'd be so glad to see Wollaton church again, but thank God — we're nearly there!'

9

There was a warm welcome as Edward and Mary dismounted outside the Blythe cottage next to the church, and Mary lost no time in hurrying out to the water butt in the back garden for a brief wash, before scuttling into the back room for a change of clothes.

Edmund Blythe invited Edward out into the rear garden, where he handed him a mug of ale and thanked him profusely for bringing his daughter home safely. Then he asked, bluntly, 'How much trouble is she in?'

Edward opted for tact. 'Far from being in any trouble, Master Blythe, I can assure you that Mary has proved herself to be a most resourceful young lady, of whom you can be justly proud.'

Edmund stared hard at Edward. 'I might be rough and ready, and with no schooling to talk about, but I'm not stupid. Our Mary's always in trouble, so tell me the truth, and don't try to cod me.'

'She *was* in trouble, certainly, Master Blythe, but in fact she saved my life a few days ago. I'm in the fortunate position of being able to overlook her previous transgressions and ensure that she is not held to account for what others did, and to which she was a largely innocent party.'

'So she's not going to go to gaol?'

'Absolutely.'

'Her mother reckons she got herself mixed up in the murder of the woman she was working for — is that right?'

'Yes, I'm afraid so. But she only thought that she was getting involved in a robbery, and as luck will have it, her testimony will save an innocent man from the hangman. That man is a good friend of mine, and I intend to ensure that your daughter redeems her past sins by helping to bring the real offender to justice.'

'That's mighty Christian of you,' Edmund conceded. 'But how do we keep her safe here until such time as you need her?'

'I'll take her home with me,' Edward replied. 'I have a household in town that is in need of additional domestic staff, and she'll be safe there. You have my word, as one father to another, and as a law officer under the Crown, that she'll come to no harm while she's under my roof.'

'I suppose I'll have to accept that,' Edmund replied gruffly, 'since you've looked after her this far. But her mother won't be happy.'

Indeed, Jane Blythe was far from happy when advised that the much-loved daughter who'd only just reappeared after weeks of worry and uncertainty would be leaving home again. Yet she soon accepted the situation when her husband explained the reasons behind it. Mary herself seemed resigned to whatever fate lay ahead of her, only too glad to put her dishonest past behind her.

Following a hearty meal that Jane insisted that they consume before their departure, and which they downed with great relish after two hungry days on the road, it was time for Edward and Mary to leave. Edward stood politely while Mary tearfully promised her parents to visit soon and stay out of any more trouble. Then they rode up the long straight path that led to Wollaton Hall, where they dismounted by the scullery door to the rear. They walked through the scullery and into the kitchen, where the cook looked up from her pastry and gave a cry of surprise.

'Welcome back, Master Mountsorrel! How is Mistress Elizabeth?'

'She is well. You may have heard that we have a young daughter now. Is the master at home today?'

'He is,' the cook replied. 'We've been told to roast a haunch of venison for dinner. But who's that standing behind you, looking all lost?'

'This is Mary Blythe, whose father is an important man in the master's coal concern. I will need to leave her in your tender care while I go in search of the master himself to report certain recent events.'

Upstairs, Edward found his employer seated in the morning room, poring over some papers. Sir Francis looked up with a frown as the usher announced him.

'About time you were back — there's been a vicious attack on a farmer's wife in Carlton while she was on her way to market with her cheeses, and the landlord of The Black Bull in Mansfield was left for dead after a riot in his taproom. The local constables seem to be without a clue as to how to proceed, and you might wish to look in on them, and at least give the appearance that we're on top of things here in the county. Remind me again of why you have been missing for four days, and advise me of the outcome, if any.'

'Excellent results in one way,' Edward reassured him, 'but a little disappointing in another.'

'Tell me the good news,' came the querulous reply.

'Not only did I find Mary Blythe and bring her safely home to her overjoyed parents, but she also gave me information that will remove the noose from around Francis Barton's neck and led me to where may be found the stolen property from the various house burglaries in recent weeks. It is in a large barn in the Derbyshire countryside and if we employ a certain deviousness we may be able to apprehend those responsible.'

'If the wench knew where the property was being hidden, then presumably she already knows the identities of those responsible?'

'Yes and no. She could no doubt identify them by sight, but she knows their names, and they are being closely protected by a local constable. He betrayed my business to them, and had it not been for the timely intervention of Mary Blythe you would now be looking for a new bailiff.'

'Your continued existence is surely not the bad news to which you referred?'

'Indeed not, but the betrayal by a local constable called Richard Grindley is. Sheriff Cockayne must be advised without delay, and we must assemble a body of men to lay siege to this barn of stolen property, while lying in wait for the thieves.'

Sir Francis glared at him in disbelief. 'You are seriously suggesting that we use Nottinghamshire men to arrest villains who are currently to be found in Derbyshire? Such would be the height of insult!'

'Surely not, if we seek Cockayne's co-operation in advance?'

'You have met Cockayne?'

'Indeed I have, and he is a most hospitable and obliging man, if I might be permitted to add my personal observation.'

'But a man, nevertheless, who delivered you into the betraying hand of one of his constables? How can we be sure that, were we to seek his in aid of our enterprise, he would not alert our quarry in advance and take steps to remove the property we seek to another location entirely?'

'You would not trust a fellow sheriff?'

'Not after what you tell me. Nor will I be prepared to share with him the praise for having put paid to the machinations of a highly skilled band of robbers.'

'But do we have enough constables of our own to bring about a successful conclusion to the matter? And is there not some requirement that we at least alert Sheriff Cockayne to what we are about?'

'In order that he may frustrate our plans? I hardly think so.'

'So we proceed with what few men I can muster, and set about resolving the matter without reference to Sheriff Cockayne?'

'Did I say that? Be under no illusion that there are enough matters that require your immediate attention within this county, without the need for you to set off again to another. You will do nothing regarding what you have learned in Derbyshire, but will seek solutions to all outstanding matters, both in the county and in Nottingham. That includes the identification and arrest of those responsible for recent house robberies.'

Edward took a deep breath in order to control his temper. 'I have already advised you that these men may be found in Derbyshire, and that if we strike without delay we may secure the return of some — if not all — of the property that they have stolen.'

Sir Francis looked sternly at Edward. 'You have your orders. And now if you will leave me in peace, I have to peruse these despatches from the chief justice concerning current policies regarding blasphemies in local churches.'

Edward turned angrily on his heel and stormed out of the room, the curses flowing freely as he took the stairs down two at a time. Willoughby expected him to bring wrongdoers to book, but was obviously not prepared to take risks, or allow his bailiff to do his job with the benefit of his years of experience. Appearances were everything, it seemed, and Edward would be required to do the impossible with one arm tied behind his back.

'Why are you in a bad mood?' Mary asked as they rode along the track into town. 'You were all cheery when we arrived and now you look like someone bit your arse.'

Edward sighed. 'I just wish people would let me get on with doing my job, instead of planting obstacles in my way.'

'Am I one of those obstacles?' she asked quietly.

'No, Mary,' he assured her, 'you're not an obstacle — you're the means by which lots of wrongs will shortly be righted.'

Back home, Mary stood back in embarrassment as Elizabeth threw her arms around the returning Edward and planted a kiss on his lips. Meg stood to one side with Margaret in her arms, looking guardedly at Mary.

'I thought some ill had befallen you,' Elizabeth complained as she regained her breath, 'since you were gone so long.'

'It would have done, had it not been for this young lady,' Edward explained as he turned to indicate Mary. 'This is Mary Blythe from Wollaton, and she saved my life. It is now our turn to save hers. I wish to give her sanctuary here until she can give such testimony as will release Francis from his current plight.'

'Doing what, exactly?' Meg asked sourly. 'And where's she going to be living?'

Edward raised his eyebrows. 'You often complain of the many duties you have to perform, Meg. Well, Mary here has experience with duties such as yours in a fine house in Cow Lane, and she can assist you. As for her living quarters, there is a spare room alongside yours next to the kitchen.'

'But I keeps things in there,' Meg pouted.

'It's not too much to ask that you make room for an assistant, is it?' Edward asked in a tone that brooked no argument. When Meg remained silent, Edward requested that she take Mary out into the garden in order that she might settle into her new quarters with the two small bags of clothing that she'd brought with her.

As they disappeared through the scullery door, Elizabeth looked apprehensively at their retreating forms. 'That house in Cow Lane,' she said. 'Is it the one in which the murder took place?'

'The very same,' Edward said. 'It was Mary who unlocked the door to the murderer, although she believed that she was only doing so to burglars. She can tell the court at Francis's trial that when she did so, he was lying unconscious because of a powder that she'd put in his wine earlier.'

'And you think that she's a suitable person to have living with us?' Elizabeth said. 'How can we be sure that she won't use the opportunity to open *this* house to burglars — or even murderers?'

'Because they're *not* her friends — at least, not any more. She's fleeing from them, and if they catch up with her they'll kill her without doubt, and I need her testimony in order to ensure that Francis is released. And she can also help me track down those who've been responsible for all those burglaries in the county that Willoughby seems to believe I should have solved by now.'

'All the same,' Elizabeth said, 'I shall not rest easily until she's gone from here.'

Meg no doubt suppressed a similar sentiment as she led Mary out into the rear garden, where local boy Robbie Bishop was engaged in splitting logs for the kitchen oven. He looked up and put down the axe.

'Who's this, then?' he asked as he looked Mary up and down. She smiled back as Meg introduced her.

Edward had followed them out and had been silently studying Robbie for a minute or two, trying to decide whether or not to entrust him with an important task. The boy was at least as tall as Edward, but much broader in the shoulder, and strong with it. When not earning a few pennies on heavy garden tasks, Robbie worked for his father Thomas Bishop, a carrier, hauling loads on and off a cart. He was not the brightest youth, but, based on experience, Edward was of the opinion that there were times when matters of the brain were best left to others, while those with the brawn were allowed to do what they did best.

'Robbie,' Edward asked, having made up his mind, 'do you think your father could spare you for a few days?'

'Prob'ly,' Robbie confirmed. 'We ain't got much work on at the moment.'

'I have a special task for you,' Edward told him. 'Mary here will be staying with us for a while, but she has made a few enemies and they may come here looking for her. I want you to keep a close eye on her. If any stranger turns up looking for her, I want you to defend her. Do you understand?'

'Of course, it'd be a pleasure,' Robbie mumbled, glancing at Mary with a flush of embarrassment on his cheeks. 'But what's she done to get 'erself enemies?'

'All you need to know is that she rescued me from a gang of ne'er-do-wells who may come looking for her in revenge. So keep close to her wherever she is.'

As Mary beamed at Robbie, Edward took her to one side. Robbie returned to chopping logs and Meg took the dishes into the back yard to rinse them at the water butt.

'Shouldn't I be helping Meg?' Mary asked.

Edward shook his head. 'That can wait. There are certain things we need to talk about first.'

'What sort of things?' Mary asked suspiciously.

Edward realised that she might have mistaken his words for some sort of prelude to a seduction, so he hastened to explain. 'First of all, your safety. There's a good chance that those ruffians you used to associate with will come looking for you, and if they do then Robbie will protect you if I'm not here.'

Mary smiled. 'If he wants to hang about me all the time, you won't hear me complaining. Meg might have other ideas, mind you.'

Edward ignored the comment. 'Secondly, there's something that's been bothering me.'

'What's that?'

'Well, when Thomas Timberlake and some of the neighbours broke into Widow Timberlake's house, they found all the doors locked — how did that come about?'

'Oh. Well, when Owen came running out into the garden to tell me that we had to take ourselves off in a hurry, he told me to lock the back door again so as nobody could come after us that way.'

'That makes sense,' said Edward. 'Now, another question, if you don't mind. Can you recall any names being mentioned when it came to your "friends"?'

'Not really,' Mary replied after a moment's thought. 'When they'd done a house, they'd come back with a list of what had been stolen — furnishings, paintings, ornaments and the like. They'd take it to some man in town who could have been

"Himself", then they'd come back with the money for their efforts.'

'You're sure that it was someone in town?'

'It must have been, because they were only gone an hour or so, and on their way back they'd obviously had time to buy a drink.'

'Any idea where they bought it from?'

'Well, sometimes we'd go to The Crusader, under the castle, because we could walk to it through the fields from Narrow Marsh. Do you know the place?'

'Only too well,' Edward replied with a grimace. 'And unless the quality of the management has improved considerably, I'll get no information from anyone there. So the only line of enquiry I have is with this man called "Himself", it would seem.'

'I've not been much help, have I?' Mary asked, crestfallen.

Edward gave her a reassuring smile. 'You have indeed, in that you've given me a lead. And now it's time I paid another visit to a man who can give me more information — a man who doesn't yet know of his change of fortune.'

10

Senior Constable Patrick Shanahan looked up from his desk inside the Guildhall as Edward entered the room.

'Good afternoon, Patrick. I'm here to visit your most important prisoner, who I hope you've been looking after?'

'We certainly are, sir, and he seems to be in good spirits. But the assize is next week, so then we'll probably be transferring Bailiff Barton to the Shire Hall cells. After that, there'll be nothing I can do for him.'

'You can leave that to me,' Edward said. 'But while I'm here, you'd better tell me if there's anything that requires my attention.'

'Not really, sir — nothing out of the ordinary. There's been a few late-night assaults up at the market, but we reckon we know who the culprit is, and when he shows his face back in Friar Row we'll have him. Then there was a riot in The Crusader a few nights since, but that had broken up afore we got there. Seems there's a band of ruffians staying down in Narrow Marsh, and we thought it best to leave them until they come out again, rather than risk a few broken heads if we went in after them.'

'They may be the same scoundrels that I'm looking for,' Edward told the constable. 'Let me know if they come out of their pigsty and I'll bring in a few reinforcements from the county.'

Francis looked up accusingly as Edward entered the cell. 'I was beginning to think you'd abandoned me,' he said mournfully.

'Such gratitude, when I have found the key to your deliverance — in more ways than one,' Edward said with a grin. 'I've found the serving girl who drugged your wine and who can tell the assize jury that she let someone else into the Timberlake house while you were insensible. It was almost certainly he who killed Agnes, but he committed a serious blunder when he failed to kill you as well. He was too clever by half when he left you to take the blame.'

Francis's eyes widened. 'You have found Mary? How did this come about?'

'By a curious coincidence,' Edward explained, as he lowered himself to the floor in order to talk more comfortably with Francis. 'Sir Francis Willoughby set me the task of finding a young woman who had been reported missing from her parents' home in Wollaton. It transpired that she was the same girl who had been in service with Agnes Timberlake on the day that she was murdered. She had been overcome with concern for her own neck, fearful that she would incur blame for the death, and I pursued her into Derbyshire.'

'And you found her?'

'Rather, she found me. I unwisely placed my trust in a local constable and told him that I was seeking a girl called Mary who had gone into hiding with a gang of villains. I then fell victim to the same poison as yourself, but Mary found me and sought my protection, which naturally I readily agreed to supply, since it will be her testimony that will save you from the hangman.'

'You have her somewhere secure?' Francis asked.

'She is at my house, being protected by a large, if slightly dull-witted, youth. But I shall, with your permission, assign two of your constables to the task.'

'Gladly! But you cannot neglect your own duties on my account.'

Edward smiled. 'I am not, as matters have transpired. This band of villains with whom Mary was associated are believed to be the same men who have been plundering some of the wealthier houses in the county in recent weeks, a matter which Sir Francis Willoughby wishes me to investigate and bring to an end. While in Derbyshire, Mary showed me the place where she claims they have hidden their ill-gotten gains. However, Willoughby will not let me engage Derbyshire constables in the task of laying siege to this building, because it would necessitate the Sheriff of Derbyshire sharing in the resulting glory. I also suspect that his constabulary is rotten with corruption, after the way in which I was betrayed, so I am here partly to seek your consent to the employment of your town constables alongside my own county men.'

Francis gave a hollow laugh. 'You seek my permission, when I am confined down here like a slug under a wet stone? Did Willoughby not give you command of the town constables?'

'Indeed he did, Francis, but I would not risk your men in a venture that might result in loss of life. But there is another way in which you might assist me.'

'Name it, and if it be within my power I shall gladly give it.'

'It seems, from what I have learned from Mary, that the man behind this burglary operation is to be found somewhere in the town. This person, referred to only as "Himself", then pays the men what I have no doubt is a mere pittance in terms of the value of those items, but sufficient for them to regard it as worth their while. They then skulk somewhere in Narrow

Marsh and convert their ill-gotten gains into liquor. Once that is all gone, they go out and plunder another house.'

Francis had been looking thoughtful as he listened to what Edward had to tell him. 'If, as you say, the stolen items are located in Derbyshire, how does this local man dispose of the plunder?'

'I have been wondering that myself,' Edward answered. 'I can only conclude that those who might be interested in acquiring the stolen property are alerted to its existence by "Himself", who then arranges for them to be escorted to Derbyshire in order to view it. Money must exchange hands at the place where the items are stored and the purchaser must then arrange to have their goods carted away.'

Francis nodded. 'How do you plan to proceed?'

'I have in mind a two-pronged approach,' Edward confided. 'The first, as I already foreshadowed, is that I take a large body of men and place them in hiding around this building in Derbyshire. When the villains arrive — whether it be with more stolen goods from their latest outrage, or escorting an eager buyer to peruse what is available — we will strike!'

'And your second approach?' Francis asked. 'Let me guess — you wish me to identify those in town who might fit the role of "Himself". Am I correct?'

'Indeed you are, Francis. Your forced confinement has in no way dimmed your wits.'

Francis grinned. 'Let me see, now. The town has several merchants who are not above suspicion when it comes to buying stolen goods, but they normally betray themselves by being too open in their endeavours to resell them. Every Saturday my men, armed with lists of recently stolen items, patrol the market stalls and make arrests. I suspect that the man you are seeking is not so stupid.'

'My thought exactly,' Edward agreed. 'The man I am seeking must be among the forefront of our leading merchants, in order to have both the contacts with wealthy men throughout the land — since he would clearly be unable to resell locally — and the wealth with which to finance such an operation. So who do we have?'

Francis frowned in concentration. 'There is Richard Gilliflower, the butcher, who supplies some of the best houses in the county. His carters would be well placed to advise him of the layout of such houses, the number and disposition of the household and suchlike. Likewise James Pringle, the furnisher, who would be a more likely suspect, given the nature of his trade. And then you will of course recall Alderman Brackenridge, who was behind the poaching of deer from the Wollaton Hall estate?'

Edward looked doubtful. 'I remain of the belief,' he said, 'that the man we are seeking is more in the way of a financier. Someone such as Josiah Greenwood, for example. He proved most unfriendly when I asked him about the gold that Agnes Timberlake had lodged with him on your account. How did you find him?'

'In truth, I only met him on two occasions,' Francis recalled. 'He is certainly a pompous ass, but surely he is already so comfortably off that he would not risk engaging a bunch of ruffians to engage in widespread acts of theft?'

'Who else, then?'

'You might try Daniel Gabriel,' Francis replied. 'He is an unscrupulous usurer who trades on the misfortunes of others. His rates are such as to cripple the average man who falls into his clutches.'

'Indeed,' Edward replied. 'And, if you recall, he is said to have loaned money to Thomas Timberlake, and it was in search of a means to repay that loan that Thomas visited Josiah Greenwood on the afternoon that his mother was murdered. That is Greenwood's account, at least, but according to Thomas he was summoned there in order to be advised of Greenwood's suspicion that you had absconded with all the money loaned to you by Agnes.'

'Little wonder that Thomas was prepared to believe that I had murdered his mother,' Francis said with a grimace. 'That would give me motive enough, were it true?'

'Do you suspect Thomas of having done the deed?' Edward asked.

Francis shrugged. 'Not now that you have advised me of the connection between the murder and the robberies of houses throughout the county. What I cannot understand is why Agnes was killed.'

Edward frowned. 'I had believed from the start that the person whose hand lay behind it was Thomas Timberlake. He resented your influence over his mother, he was in urgent need of money, he stood to gain by her death, the weapon used to kill her came from his own workshop, and he was conveniently elsewhere — with Josiah Greenwood — when she was killed, having arranged for the only possible witness, his apprentice Ralph Meadows, to be distracted by visitors. And, of course, he lost no time in pointing the finger at you when circumstances suggested that it might have been you who committed the crime.'

Francis looked equally confused. 'If it be the case that whoever murdered Agnes was one of these villains who have been burglarising houses, then Thomas would also have to be the person behind the burglaries, or would have hired them to carry out the murder,' he pointed out. 'But if he was pursuing such a profitable line in crime, why would he need his mother's fortune?'

Edward frowned. 'I must speak more with Ralph Meadows regarding that fateful afternoon. And I must enquire of Daniel Gabriel whether he was pressuring Thomas for the repayment of the loan, if any such loan actually existed, of course.'

'I wish I could offer my assistance,' Francis replied ruefully, 'since you have worked so hard on my behalf.'

'That reminds me — your assize is set for next week. In the next few days, in anticipation of that, you will be transferred to a cell in the Shire Hall. I shall leave word that yours is to be one of those above the ground, with a high window that adjoins the rear yard, so that you may at least enjoy some fresh air.'

'And we must pray for little wind,' Francis said as Edward bid him farewell.

Edward opted to make his first visit of that afternoon to the workshop in Cow Lane. When he arrived, it appeared that Thomas Timberlake was in the process of moving into his late mother's house, judging by the comings and goings of various carters' labourers, heaving furniture through the front door, and being ordered about in a loud and critical voice by Thomas himself. Edward took his opportunity and scurried down the alley to the workshop, where Ralph Meadows was chipping carefully at the bust of what looked like a Greek god.

Meadows looked up and smiled at Edward. 'Thanks for not callin' out and makin' my 'and slip. This here's the delicate bit and if I get it wrong the whole bloody thing'll be ruined, and the master'll kick my arse from one end of this workshop to the other.'

Edward grinned. 'I just need to ask you a question about the day that Widow Timberlake was murdered.'

'What's that, then?' Meadows asked.

'Two men came into the workshop that day, one of them wishing to examine the statue outside — which I see still hasn't found a customer — while the other one remained here. Do you recall that?'

'Yes.'

'Did your master tell you to expect them? Or did they appear unexpectedly?'

'I didn't expect 'em,' the lad replied without hesitation. 'I was a little worried, because the master normally speaks to customers. But they said they were only lookin'. Does that answer your question?'

'It does, thank you,' Edward said. He bid the apprentice farewell and strolled back down the alley, deep in thought.

If Thomas Timberlake hadn't deliberately sent two men to the workshop to distract Ralph, then this made it unlikely that he had been behind the murder of his mother. But that wasn't to say that Thomas hadn't arranged their arrival behind Ralph's back. At least he'd managed to unearth evidence that would prove Francis's innocence, but it would be a bonus if he could identify who *had* been the murderer.

His next call was at the business premises of Daniel Gabriel, which was situated behind the imposing colonnades of Long Row, conveniently located on the north side of the Market Place, where merchants might be tempted inside to negotiate some sort of temporary cash loan ahead of a day's trading.

A richly dressed attendant announced Edward's entry, and a grey-haired man with a distinguished air and aquiline nose held out his hand. Edward didn't so much shake Daniel Gabriel's hand as have his own hand firmly gripped in a cold maw that felt like a dried fish.

'I don't believe we've had occasion to meet,' Gabriel said coldly. 'I assume that you are not here in your official capacity, so it must be the need for temporary financial accommodation that brings you here.'

'It *is* official business that brings me here,' Edward replied formally.

'You appreciate that all my financial dealings are enshrouded with a confidentiality that I extend to all my business associates?' Gabriel warned.

'Even those who've defaulted on their loans?'

If Gabriel was thrown by this blunt enquiry it didn't show on his face. 'I am fortunate that very few find themselves in that situation.'

'As indeed are they, from what I hear of your methods of collection,' Edward replied with distaste.

Gabriel's lips twisted in a snarl. 'Your meaning?'

'I will not prevaricate,' Edward replied. 'You had occasion to loan money to the alabaster merchant Thomas Timberlake?'

'As I have already indicated, Master Mountsorrel, my business affairs are confidential.'

'And that loan remained unpaid, and overdue, on the day that his mother was murdered?'

'You clearly suffer from a defect in hearing, young man,' Gabriel replied as he reached for a bell on his desk. 'You may enquire all you wish regarding a paltry thirty-pound accommodation, and my response will not vary; namely that all such matters are those of gentlemanly discretion between myself and the borrower.'

'You have already confirmed what I already knew,' Edward said triumphantly. 'I had been advised that the amount involved was thirty pounds, and you have just supplied the corroboration.'

Gabriel rang the bell and the door behind his desk opened with such alacrity that Edward could only conclude that the two burly men who emerged through it had been listening intently for the signal.

'Bailiff Mountsorrel is just leaving,' Gabriel told them. 'And if he offers no resistance then he may do so with his limbs intact.'

At least he lived up to his reputation, Edward consoled himself as he stood on the pavement in Long Row. The angle of the sun suggested that he had a couple of hours yet before Elizabeth would demand his attendance at the supper table, so he cut across the busy market place and allowed his horse to weave its way through the crowded thoroughfare of Bridlesmith Gate and down into Low Pavement. He hitched the bridle to a railing and walked into Patrick Shanahan's office for the second time that day.

'Patrick,' Edward said lightly, in an effort to make his request sound like an invitation to partake in an exciting adventure. 'Could you name a few of your constables who'd welcome a jaunt out into Derbyshire for a day or two?'

'What for?' Shanahan replied cautiously.

'I have reason to suspect that inside a farm building not two days' ride from here can be found a large quantity of items stolen from certain wealthy houses throughout the county.'

'So it's a county matter?' came the blunt response, but Edward had anticipated that.

'In essence, yes, but I believe that those responsible for the thefts are to be found here in town. I will of course be employing all the county constables at my disposal, but I thought that some additional manpower from the town might prove advantageous. Of course, the town constables are currently mine to command, but I'd prefer to lead volunteers.'

'I'll ask around,' Shanahan replied, 'but we've got plenty of work of our own, as you'll be aware.'

'I would be obliged if you would.' Edward turned to go and almost collided with Constable Weldon as he raced in, out of breath and sweating.

'I thought that was your horse outside, sir, so I came directly here to fetch you, begging your pardon and all.'

'Fetch me to where, exactly?'

'Your house, sir. Leastways, your garden. There's been a fight and I'm not sure who to arrest.'

11

The scene that met Edward as he hurried into his rear garden was chaotic. A large, bearded man lay on his back in the centre of the lawn, yelling, while a determined-looking Robbie Bishop sat astride his chest, rhythmically landing blows on his face as if he were playing a drum. Two town constables were warning Robbie that if he didn't desist he would be taken into custody — although neither seemed eager to attempt to do so — while Mary Blythe was urging Robbie to greater effort with such blandishments as, 'Turn his nose into a dumpling!'

Meg was standing fearfully at the kitchen door watching the proceedings and Edward enquired after Elizabeth. 'She's inside the house, Master,' Meg told him, 'since she reckoned that this were no sight for the bubby to see — and quite right too! Can you not get him to stop?'

Edward strode over to Robbie. 'You can get off him now, Robbie, and let the constables take him into custody, assuming that there's good reason to do so.'

'The villain came after Mary with a knife!' Robbie growled as he rolled off the man and got to his feet.

Mary rushed over and threw her arms around Robbie. 'That's Owen Drinkwater,' she told Edward. 'I was standing by the kitchen door with Meg when he came for me with that knife.' She indicated the far corner of the lawn, where a glint in the setting sun betrayed the location of a large blade.

Edward looked across at the bearded man. 'Master Drinkwater? Is that your *real* name?'

Owen muttered an oath and one of the constables twisted his arm halfway up his back so that he was barely standing on tiptoe.

'Henry Sly!' the man yelled. 'Now get these oafs off me!'

Edward ignored him and nodded at the two constables. 'Take him to the Guildhall and put him in a cell. And if he gives you any trouble on the way, you have my authority to twist his arm again.'

A cursing Sly was bundled out through the rear gate and up the side path onto Whitefriars Lane.

Edward turned to Robbie, who was still half hidden by Mary's encircling arms. 'Well done, Robbie — that was very brave of you.'

'It wasn't anything special,' Robbie replied modestly. 'But no-one is going to take a blade to Mary while I'm around.'

'Are you all right, Mary? Meg?' Edward asked and the two young women nodded in unison.

Indoors, the house appeared deserted and an anxious Edward took the stairs two at a time as he called out Elizabeth's name. He found her in their bedchamber, little Margaret snuggled into her chest. She looked up, pale-faced, as Edward entered the room.

'That was awful!' she whispered. 'Thank goodness Robbie was here, else poor Mary would be a mere memory. You can't let her stay here after that, surely?'

'Why not? Robbie's proved his worth as her bodyguard and if it makes you feel any easier, I'll get two of the town constables to stand guard — one in front of the house and the other at the garden gate.'

'You don't seriously intend to leave us all alone again, after what just happened?' Elizabeth protested.

'I need to go to the Guildhall and interview that man Sly. If my suspicions are correct, he was the one who murdered Agnes Timberlake. The assize starts next Monday, and I think that Francis's will be the first trial on the list, since it's a case of murder.'

'You promised to take us to Ashby this coming weekend,' Elizabeth reminded him tersely.

Edward spread his arms wide in exasperation. 'You cannot seriously hold me to a promise that I made in all good faith without knowing that within days my duties to my office, not to mention the duty that I owe to my friend, would cast me into a situation in which I would need to beg to be excused from it?'

'I have never known a time when your duties did not sway you from honouring your obligations to those who should be the nearest and dearest to you. In case you have forgotten, they are your wife and daughter.'

Edward sighed. 'We have been married barely two years, and in that time we have visited your parents more than once ...'

'And if you wish to remain married — to me, at least — then we must visit them once again. This weekend.'

'Francis Barton will hang unless I can make the assize jury aware of what Mary Blythe can tell them regarding the events attending the death of Agnes Timberlake,' Edward replied hotly. 'And Mary herself may still be in danger. We need to stay here and keep an eye on her.'

Elizabeth looked thoughtful. 'Both of those things depend upon Mary's safety, do they not?'

'Yes.'

'Then our dilemma is easily resolved. We will take Mary with us. Having been a lady's maid myself for so many years, it will make a welcome change to travel with a lady's maid of my own.'

Edward was about to protest when the logic of what Elizabeth suggested hit home. Today was Thursday, and he had to keep Mary safe until the assize began on the following Monday. If they travelled to Ashby, less than a full day's ride south into Leicestershire, and returned on Sunday evening, then Mary's safety could be assured and she would be available as a witness in Francis's cause on Monday.

'It shall be as you wish,' he said.

Elizabeth looked surprised. 'We can ride to Ashby on Saturday?'

'No — we will leave tomorrow, provided that it will be in order for me to ride back here with Mary on Sunday, after dinner. We can leave Robbie here to guard the house, and Meg, which will free up two constables to go about their normal business. Then, once I return, Robbie can accompany Mary to the Shire Hall when I produce her as a witness in Francis's trial.'

'I hope that you will not acquaint my parents with Mary's true character? They live under this happy illusion that my husband leads an honourable life, devoted to me and our daughter, and ever attentive to our needs.'

Edward chuckled as he went back downstairs to advise Meg of their plans.

Meg scowled. 'At least I may look forward to some sleep at last.'

'You need not have any fear,' Edward said. 'Robbie will remain here to guard you and the house. Perhaps he might be persuaded to occupy Mary's bed while she is away.'

Meg shot him a withering look. 'It is because he *already* occupies her bed that I cannot get any sleep!'

Henry Sly looked up sullenly as the turnkey unlocked the cell door and let Edward in. Edward requested that the turnkey leave the torch in the wall bracket as he looked down at his prisoner.

'Why did you murder Agnes Timberlake, and on whose orders?' Edward demanded.

'I didn't murder her, and your officers can twist my arm all they like — it's better than getting hung for nothing.'

'I have a witness who says that she opened the door of the Timberlake house for you.'

'Mary Blythe opened the door for the killer, right enough, but that wasn't me. My job was to distract the lad in the workshop while Job Manners went into the house to kill the widow.'

'So you admit that the reason you and this Job Manners were both at the house was to murder Agnes Timberlake?'

'Yes, but I wasn't the one who did it.'

'But you assisted the man who did. That means that you'll hang with him. Unless…'

'Unless what?'

'Unless you tell me who hired the pair of you to do it.'

Sly shook his head. 'If I told you, I'd be as good as dead anyway. That bloke doesn't think twice about doing away with those who cross him.'

'You deliberately befriended Mary Blythe, didn't you, so that she could be persuaded to drug her mistress's wine and let some of your men into the house?'

Sly glared at him, but remained silent.

'So if, as you say,' Edward continued, 'it was Job Manners who entered the house to do the deed, how come you left by the back door to collect Mary Blythe from the garden?'

'Because it all went wrong when the woman's son came home earlier than expected. We were told that he'd be at a meeting, but that must have ended early, because I was still standing in the alley by the house when all this shouting started up at the front of the house, and the lad I was distracting was called to go and help break down the door. So I ran back through the workshop and into the house. It was empty, so Job must have taken to his heels over the back fence. I went to find Mary, we locked the back door, and then we made a run for it through the garden and down the other lane. There was that much fuss and carry-on out the front of the house that nobody saw us slip away.'

'Where is Job Manners now?'

Sly shrugged. 'No idea. We have lots of places where we can hide away when we need to.'

'And you're not prepared to tell me who paid you both to do the job that ended in the death of Agnes Timberlake?'

'Like I said, it's more than my life's worth. I'll tell you this much, though — it wasn't the man who normally pays us for the burglaries.'

'Not "Himself", you mean?'

'You can ask Job Manners — if you ever catch up with him, that is.'

'Then I'd better set about doing that, hadn't I?' Edward said. 'As for you, you'll be held here on a charge of burglary and the attempted murder of Mary Blythe.'

12

Edward assisted Elizabeth out of the carriage and lost no time in handing Margaret over to her cooing grandparents. Mary lifted down two large travelling bags, then stood politely as she was introduced as Elizabeth's new maid. They were grouped outside the former gatehouse to the Ashby estate of the Hastings family, whom Edwin and Catherine Porter had faithfully served until their retirement to the grace-and-favour home that had been theirs for some years now.

'She's grown,' Catherine commented as she looked down lovingly at Margaret. 'Mind you,' she continued, looking slightly accusingly at Edward, 'we haven't seen her for a while. Is she walking yet?'

As they chatted they moved into the house. Edward, Elizabeth and Margaret had been allocated the only bedchamber, Edwin and Catherine insisting that they would be happy enough sleeping in the main room, next to the fireplace that was already being employed as the warm summer began to give way to chill autumn evenings. Mary was allocated a space in the small stable that came with the gatehouse, which she would be required to share not only with their three horses, but also the old mare that the elderly couple kept, more out of charity than any need for transport.

Any ill humour that Mary might have experienced regarding her temporary accommodation was swiftly dissipated by an invitation from Catherine to assist her in making a parsnip pie for dinner, which was gladly washed down with beer, after which Elizabeth and her mother sat with baby Margaret while

Mary took to unpacking what seemed to be Elizabeth's entire wardrobe.

Edwin invited Edward to take the air in the long vegetable garden that he'd painstakingly created over the years, and once they were out of earshot the reason for the invitation became clear.

'What's going on, Edward? Whoever that lass Mary is, she's no lady's maid. She's far too rough and ready, and I've seen enough ladies' maids in my time to know the difference. The wife noticed it immediately. No doubt you know your own business, and I'm not asking you to betray any secrets, but can you put our minds at rest?'

Edward realised that there was no need for secrecy. 'Of course, Edwin. Mary is an important witness in a trial that starts at the assize on Monday, which is why I'll be riding back with her after dinner on Sunday, leaving my wife and daughter here with you. There are some bad people who would like nothing more than to silence her, and they've made one attempt already. We were long overdue a visit to Ashby, as Elizabeth has recently reminded me, and I'd be a lot happier knowing that she's safely out of harm's way here in the countryside. I need to undertake several journeys into Derbyshire in the near future, in the course of my duties, so if it's not imposing too much, I would be grateful if Elizabeth and Margaret could stay here with you for a week or two.'

'That's no hardship at all, and I thank you for your candour,' Edwin assured him. 'Let's go and help ourselves to some more of that beer, shall we?'

Sunday came round all too quickly. 'Why are you leaving us here when you take Mary back into town?' Elizabeth asked Edward as they lay in their bed ahead of rising for breakfast,

Margaret snuffling quietly in a makeshift cot beside them.

'For your safety, of course,' Edward replied. 'Aside from Francis's trial, I also need to journey into Derbyshire on business for Willoughby, and you'd only complain at my absence if you were left alone in Whitefriars Lane.'

'You're sure there's no other reason?'

Edward frowned. 'What other reason could there be?'

Elizabeth hesitated, then murmured, 'Mary.'

It took Edward a moment to realise that she wasn't alluding to the upcoming trial. 'You don't really believe that I'd … well, you know … with Mary?'

'Well, she's a willing and eager woman, and, well, according to Meg she's already been going to it with poor old Robbie.'

'"Poor old Robbie" probably thinks he's died and gone to Heaven. But while she's busy with him, she's hardly likely to try her charms on me, is she? You know I only have eyes for you.'

Elizabeth smiled and wrapped her arms around him.

An hour after dinner, following several tearful farewells, Edward and Mary set out on the track that led north-east, via the villages of Kegworth and Long Eaton, towards Nottingham.

'Do you think Robbie'd like parsnip pie?' Mary asked after they had ridden some way in silence. 'He's got some growing in your garden, hasn't he?'

'Parsnips? Or pies?' Edward joked, and Mary giggled. Edward thought he could guess where her mind was wandering. 'You've taken quite a shine to Robbie, haven't you?' His quick sideways glance was enough to see the colour rise in her cheeks.

'Yes, and I think that he quite likes me. He's just the kind of man I'd like to settle down with.'

'He's still a young lad,' Edward reminded her.

'Robbie's kind and gentle, but strong when he needs to be. One day he'll inherit his dad's business — then who knows?'

'I might be able to find employment for him as a constable,' Edward told her as he gave voice to a thought that had been forming ever since he'd seen how Robbie had dealt with Henry Sly. 'But before that day arrives, and before you think of settling down, don't forget that you have to appear before a jury and tell them about the day that your mistress was murdered.'

'Do you promise that I won't go to gaol?' Mary whispered fearfully.

'I already made you that promise,' Edward said. 'And tomorrow you must keep yours.'

13

The upper room of the Shire Hall was already crowded with people, all keen to view the town bailiff, Francis Barton, on trial for murder. Edward pushed his way to the front, followed closely by Mary, with Robbie by her side just in case. Sheriff Thomas Drury looked up briefly from the parchment roll in front of him, then shook his head sadly.

'I never thought that I would be called upon to send my own bailiff to the gallows,' he told Edward gloomily. 'But the testimony from these witnesses can only lead to one conclusion, unless you bring me happier tidings.'

'Indeed I do,' Edward replied, beckoning Mary forward. 'This is the servant employed in the house of Agnes Timberlake on the afternoon of her murder, Mary Blythe. She can tell the jury that shortly before the dreadful deed was done, she tampered with the wine Francis and Agnes were drinking by adding an ingredient that rendered them both insensible, and that she then unlocked a door that gave access to the house from the adjoining workshop, in order to grant admission to the true murderer.'

Drury looked at Mary through narrowed eyes. 'If she be implicated in the death, then why is she not in custody awaiting a presenting jury?'

'Because she believed that she was opening the house to a mere burglar, and had no foreknowledge of a planned murder.'

'Even assuming that she convinces the jury that Francis had been rendered insensible,' Drury persisted, 'how do we account for the blood on his sword?'

'I have two more witnesses,' Edward replied. 'One is an apothecary who will speak to the effects of valerian when placed in a fusion of wine, and the other is the physician who examined the corpse of Agnes Timberlake, and who will state that the wounds she suffered came not from Francis's sword.'

'Do you yourself intend to advise the jury of the results of your enquiries?' Drury asked.

Edward looked uncertain. 'Would that be permitted? I know not of how matters proceed before a petty jury, having only ever appeared at presentments.'

Drury gave him a wry smile. 'There is only one person who may object if an accused person wishes others to be called in his defence, and that is me. If I offer no objection, His Honour is unlikely to interfere. Particularly not Justice Fairbanks, who will be Francis's judge today. He is renowned for his pursuit of fairness in criminal trials, although this does not seem to have blighted his career.'

There was an excited murmur from the crowd and Edward turned to see the trapdoor in the dock had opened with a bang. Francis appeared through it, each arm in the grip of a turnkey. He was ordered to sit on the bench in front of the trapdoor, and a chain was passed through the manacles that encircled his ankles, then firmly knocked into place inside the floor restraints. Edward made his way through the watching crowd to lean on the rail in front of the prisoner.

'Be of good cheer, my dear friend,' Edward smiled encouragingly. 'I have brought witnesses.'

'My thanks, for what use they may prove to be,' Francis replied wearily. 'At least I was allowed to wash.'

There was a loud knocking from the far side of the chamber and a door opened to reveal a liveried flunkey, dressed as if for a royal pageant, followed closely behind by a tall man festooned in the red and ermine robes of a justice of the queen's bench.

'All those having business before this court, let them now approach and they shall be heard. God save the Queen,' the flunkey regaled the crowd.

Justice Fairbanks arranged himself on the padded bench like a hen settling on eggs.

Sheriff Drury turned to face His Lordship and announced his rank and title. 'I have the matter of the Queen versus Francis Barton, should Your Lordship be graciously willing to preside over same as the first in your list. The charge is one of murder, and the prisoner has been brought into court.'

Justice Fairbanks nodded his agreement, and another court official, not so grandly attired as the one who had accompanied the judge into the courtroom, set about calling the names of those summoned to serve on the petty jury. Once all twelve had acknowledged their names and stepped forward, they took their place on a cramped bench to the side of the courtroom.

Drury read out the charge, then looked across the courtroom at the town bailiff. 'What say you, Francis Barton? Do you plead guilty or not guilty?'

Francis rose as instructed by one of his gaolers. 'Not Guilty,' he said in a slightly croaky voice, then sat down again. With the leave of the judge, Drury began calling his witnesses.

The first to appear was an indignant Thomas Timberlake, who told the jury of his mother's decision to lend her entire fortune to the prisoner, to be held under his instruction in the vaults of the business premises of Josiah Greenwood. 'Francis Barton seduced her,' Thomas continued, 'and thereafter set about obtaining access to the entire monetary legacy left to her by my late father, whose business I inherited on his death. Despite frequent solicitations, both to my mother and Francis

Barton, I was unable to secure an advance on the inheritance that one day would be mine, in order that I might expand my business and thereby benefit us both.'

He went on to recount how, on the afternoon of his mother's death, he had been summoned by Josiah Greenwood to a meeting at the latter's business premises in order that Greenwood might convey to him, in confidence, his suspicion that Francis had embezzled the entire sum held at his disposal.

At this point Justice Fairbanks raised a hand in an indication that Thomas should pause in his evidence. As Thomas came to an uncertain halt, the judge asked, 'You say that this money had been loaned to the prisoner by your mother?'

'Yes, sir.'

'If that be the case, then he was presumably entitled to do with it as he wished, and for some purpose of his own, was he not?'

'Indeed, sir, but I was also advised by Greenwood that my mother had requested that Barton give an accounting to her of the entire sum loaned, and Greenwood was aware that none of the amount in question — over a thousand pounds — remained available.'

'Very well — please continue.'

Thomas Timberlake told the court that, on the fateful day, he had a supper appointment with both his mother and Francis, and intended to challenge Francis with what he had been told by Greenwood. But upon reaching his mother's house in Cow Lane he discovered that the house was locked, and realised that he had forgotten to bring his key. After he had knocked for several minutes, without success, he had grown apprehensive for his mother's safety had called upon a some neighbours, along with his workshop apprentice, to force open the front door. A search of the house revealed the naked and bloodied body of his mother lying in her bedchamber. Standing alongside the bed, splattered with blood and clad in only his hose, was Francis Barton. A physician had been summoned, and had confirmed that Agnes was dead, whereupon the constables were called, and Francis was taken in charge.

Once again Justice Fairbanks raised his hand, and once again Thomas halted in his account of the events of that day.

'Did the prisoner make any attempt to escape?' the judge asked.

Thomas shook his head. 'No, sir,' he replied. 'He seemed overawed by the enormity of what he had done, and was staring in disbelief at his own wicked handiwork.'

'And did he make any admission of guilt at this time?'

'No, sir.'

'If he made no admission, how can it be said that it *was* his handiwork?'

'A sword was found at the side of the bed, on which was found some blood. Barton admitted that the sword was his, although he was unable to recall how it had come to be bloodstained.'

'Was anyone else found to be in the house?' the judge asked.

'No, sir. And what is more, sir,' he added with obvious relish, 'all the doors to the house were locked, including the front door to which I had been unable to gain access.'

'Servants?' Fairbanks queried, to be met with another shake of the head.

'My mother was very frugal in her household, sir, and had only two indoor servants — the cook Nell, who was visiting family that day, and a girl called Mary, who has not been seen since the day of the murder.'

'Might she have been complicit in your mother's death?'

'It would not surprise me, sir, since she was a slovenly wench.'

Edward sensed Mary bristle with anger beside him.

Timberlake completed his testimony and was told that he was free to go. The next witness was the physician, James Morton, who confirmed that he had been called to the Timberlake house on the day that Agnes's body had been discovered, and had remained for long enough to confirm that she was dead. Morton was followed by a town constable, Robert Reevers, who had helped convey the corpse to the room under the Guildhall, where the deceased were kept pending their interment in the graveyard of the family's choice. He had also been required to take Francis Barton into custody, and had handed him over to a turnkey for incarceration in one of the cells.

'This man was your superior officer, was he not?' Justice Fairbanks asked. When Reevers confirmed that this was the case, the judge asked, 'Did you not find it distressful, to be locking up your own bailiff on such a serious charge?'

'I does me duty, sir,' Reevers replied stoically, and this was the close of the case for the prosecution.

It was rapidly approaching midday and Justice Fairbanks looked hopefully down at Sheriff Drury. 'Have we time for another matter from the list before we adjourn for dinner, once the jury announce their finding on the current one?'

Drury coughed politely. 'The current matter is not quite over, Your Lordship. I am advised that there are several additional witnesses.'

'I thought I heard you announce that you had called all your witnesses?'

'You did, Your Lordship. These additional witnesses are being brought by the prisoner, with your leave, of course. I may say that in the circumstances I have no objection.'

'Who are they, and what have they to say?'

'Perhaps I might allow that question to be answered by my acting town bailiff, Edward Mountsorrel, Your Lordship? He is also the county bailiff, but has been assuming town duties until the Barton matter has been concluded.'

'And is he in court?'

'I am, Your Lordship,' Edward announced boldly as he stepped forward from the crowd of spectators.

'You realise that it is unusual for a prisoner to be allowed to call witnesses? It only delays proceedings,' Justice Fairbanks said.

'Proceedings are perhaps best delayed, if we are to get to the truth of a matter,' he suggested, and was relieved when the judge gave a wry smile.

'Would I be correct in suggesting that you have been investigating this matter for yourself, Master Mountsorrel?'

'You would indeed, Your Lordship. Francis Barton and I have been colleagues for several years, and he is also a good friend. I refused to believe that he is capable of that of which he is accused, and so I commenced enquiries of my own.'

'Perhaps if you would give us the benefit of a summary of your enquiries, and their findings, then we may assess whether or not it is appropriate to call further witnesses. You would be prepared to swear the witness oath, in full knowledge of the penalties for perjury?'

'Indeed I would, Your Lordship.'

'Very well — please step up to the witness stand and swear the oath.'

Having sworn to tell the truth before God, and conscious of all that hung — literally — on what he had to reveal, Edward took a deep breath and began.

'As I have already explained, Your Lordship, I found it impossible to accept that Francis Barton had so brutally slaughtered someone for whom he held a deep affection. Francis had made no secret of the fact — to me, anyway — that he and the deceased Agnes Timberlake were lovers. Such was her regard for him that she had loaned him her entire inheritance, lodged in the vaults of a local trader, for reasons that need not concern this court. I mention that only in order to demonstrate the depth of the mutual regard between Agnes Timberlake and Francis Barton, although I add that this loan was for the duration of Agnes's life, so that Barton could not have benefitted from her death. Quite the reverse, in fact.'

'I think that you've made your point, Master Mountsorrel,' Justice Fairbanks responded drily. 'You could not believe your friend to be guilty of the murder of this lady, so how did you go about your enquiries?'

'I began, Your Lordship, with the question of whether or not anyone else could have gained access to the house while Master Barton and Agnes Timberlake were upstairs in the bedchamber. You will recall the evidence that all the doors to the house were locked?'

'Yes, yes — get on with it.'

'Well, Master Barton advised me that Agnes Timberlake herself had been responsible for locking the doors from the inside, so naturally I pursued the possibility that one of the doors had subsequently been opened by someone else, from the inside, in order to grant admission to someone waiting on the other side in order to enter the house and commit the deed.'

'And?'

'I learned that shortly before the fatal act, two men had diverted the attention of the apprentice employed in the workshop adjacent to the house, which shares an adjoining door. This adjoining door was one of those found to be locked after the event, of course. But close questioning of the apprentice concerned — who in my opinion remains entirely blameless in this matter — revealed that he had been kept occupied in the lane adjoining the workshop by one man, while the other remained inside the workshop. While there, this man would have had access to all manner of tools such as are employed in the carving of alabaster — Master Timberlake's trade. I later obtained confirmation from the physician, James Morton, who you will recall gave evidence earlier, and who remains available to give further testimony should Your Lordship deem it appropriate, that one of these tools was more likely to have been the cause of the wounds on the deceased's body than Francis Barton's sword.'

'I think we will need to hear that additional testimony, Master Mountsorrel.'

'Now or later, Your Lordship?'

'Later. Your story has me intrigued, and I would hear more of it.'

Greatly heartened, Edward continued. 'There remained the curious matter of how the murderer gained access to the house, and how Francis Barton came to be — as he advised me — insensible when someone so cruelly attacked Agnes Timberlake as she lay by his side. He himself remained unharmed, which of course resulted in the finger of suspicion pointing at him. But this led me to speculate that Francis had been spared in order that he might take the blame, and be hanged for the atrocity. But how had he come to offer no resistance to the attack on Agnes, and to have no memory of it even occurring? One suggestion, of course, is a potion of some sort — one that overcomes the senses.'

'Valerian, perhaps?' the judge ventured.

Edward nodded vigorously. 'The very same, Your Lordship. I have arranged for a local apothecary to attend in order to testify as to the qualities of valerian — that is unless Your Honour is prepared to accept the possibility that it could have had such consequences as I have outlined?'

'Yes, I am,' Fairbanks replied shortly. 'So that is one witness less. But how was this potion administered, and by whom?'

'I had hoped that this would prove to be the same person who unlocked the door between the house and the workshop — from the inside. Someone, in short, who was prevailed upon to take both actions, perhaps unaware that murder was the ultimate objective, and not a mere burglary.'

'And you have identified such a person?' Fairbanks asked, leaning forward on the front panel of his bench like an eager spectator at a cock-fight.

Edward nodded. 'I both identified and located her, Your Lordship, and she is here today to testify. Her name is Mary Blythe, and she was the house servant referred to by Master Timberlake in his evidence'.

'You have her in custody?'

'No, Your Lordship. She is here of her own free will, anxious to see justice done in this case.'

'Then perhaps we should hear what she can tell us. Please step forward and take the oath, Mistress Blythe.'

Mary swallowed hard and stepped forward warily to take the oath.

'You realise that the oath you have just taken means that if you tell a lie, you can be severely punished?' Justice Fairbanks asked.

Mary turned pale as she replied 'Yes,' in a small voice.

'Very well, then. Please tell the court what you know of this matter.'

'Well, sir,' Mary began, 'I was working for the Widow Timberlake, who was very good to me. She was in the habit of entertaining Master Barton, and she always asked me to leave the house while they — well, when they were doing the business, if you get my drift?'

'I think we can all accept that the deceased and the prisoner were in a relationship,' the judge instructed her. 'Your mistress dismissed you from the house on the afternoon of her death, you say?'

'Yes, she did, except I came back inside and unlocked the door to the workshop while they were upstairs.'

'And why did you do that?'

'Well, I'd met this nice fellow called Owen — except it turned out that he wasn't all that nice after all, and I discovered later that Owen wasn't even his real name. Well, me and Owen were planning on getting married. I found out that he and his friends were robbing houses, and they asked me to help them rob the one I was working in.'

'What happened next?'

'I dropped some powder into the wine that the mistress and Master Barton were drinking, so that they wouldn't hear anything when the house was being robbed.'

'Have you any idea what this powder was?'

Mary shook her head. 'It was a funny brown colour. I'd been told to make sure that it was stirred well into the wine, so that they wouldn't notice the taste.'

'Pray continue,' said the judge.

'Well, I put this powder in the wine and delivered it to the mistress. Then the mistress said I was free to go back to my room out behind the kitchen in the back garden, and come back when it was time to serve the supper.'

'But you let yourself back into the house before then?'

'Yes. I came back a little while later, and put my ear to the keyhole. I couldn't hear anything — not a squeak — so I let myself back in with the key I'd been given by the mistress, and I crept through the house and unlocked the door that leads to the workshop next door.'

'When you let yourself back into the house, did you hear any sounds from upstairs? Any cries of pain? Any pleas for mercy? Anything to indicate that your mistress was being attacked?'

'No, there was nothing. It was like a graveyard up there.'

'So when you unlocked the door — and think very carefully before you answer — who was it that you let into the house?'

Mary shrugged. 'I've no idea. I just legged it through the house and back out to the garden. I just assumed it was Owen who I'd let in, but I didn't hang about to find out.'

'But did you see this man Owen at the house that day?'

'Yeah — he came into the garden and got the key off me so he could lock the back door again. Then he told me that we needed to get out of Nottingham, and he dragged me away.'

'Why did he do that?'

'Well, there was a lot of noise coming from the street, and Owen told me the mistress had been done in, and if we didn't run for it we'd get the blame.'

'So you left with him?'

Mary nodded. 'Then a couple of weeks later, Bailiff Mountsorrel come looking for me in Derbyshire, and promised that I'd be safe if I come back with him to Nottingham.

Perhaps it's as well I did, because Owen came after me with a knife, and the young man I'm seeing now jumped on him and half killed him, until the bailiff had him locked up.'

Justice Fairbanks looked across at Edward in the front row of spectators and asked, 'Is this person calling himself "Owen" now safely in custody, Bailiff Mountsorrel?'

'He is indeed, Your Lordship,' Edward confirmed. 'And his true name is Henry Sly. He will be charged with the attempted murder of Mistress Blythe here, and perhaps something more serious in due course.'

'Very well. Witness, is there anything else you can tell us about this matter?'

'No, sir,' Mary said with a tear in her eye. 'Only that I'm very sorry for what happened to Mistress Timberlake.'

'Very well, thank you for coming forward to tell what you know. You may now stand down. Now, Master Mountsorrel, may we hear again from the physician? I'd like to hear his testimony regarding the nature of the wounds inflicted on the deceased.'

James Morton stepped once more into the space allocated to witnesses and took the oath. His face expressed surprise when they came, not from Sheriff Drury, or even Bailiff Mountsorrel, but the trial judge.

'Master Morton, what can you tell us about the wounds you found on the body of Agnes Timberlake?'

'There were plenty of them, Your Lordship, and several of them would have been more than enough to cause death on their own. There was blood all over the body, so it was difficult to be precise, but I would say no less than twelve blows in all.'

'We've heard that a sword was found in the bedchamber where the body lay. Could that have been employed to inflict those wounds?'

'Very unlikely, in my professional judgment. Whatever was used to kill the victim was more robust than a sword blade, which is too thin and fragile to account for the broad wounds that I observed on the corpse.'

'Have you any idea what this might have been?'

'Yes, Your Lordship. Bailiff Mountsorrel called at my house and showed me some sort of tool employed in the carving of alabaster, and I agreed with him that this would have been a more likely agency of death than a sword.'

Fairbanks looked at Edward enquiringly. 'I don't suppose…?' he asked.

Edward reached into his doublet pocket and removed the chisel. 'This is the tool, Your Lordship. It is from Thomas Timberlake's workshop.'

'If you'd be so good as to show it to the witness.'

Edward stepped forward and handed the chisel to Morton, who studied it for a moment. 'This is the same tool you showed me before. It is certainly more likely to have inflicted those wounds than any sword blade,' he confirmed.

'Nevertheless, blood *was* found on the sword blade that the prisoner has admitted was his, was it not?' Justice Fairbanks prompted him.

'Indeed, there was some blood on it, but hardly enough to account for it having been used to inflict all those wounds. And in my experience, wounds inflicted with a sword tend to cause blood to spurt all the way up the blade, even as far as the hilt. I found nothing of that nature on the sword I was shown.'

'We have heard that the prisoner had blood on his hose. Could that have occurred when he attacked the victim?'

'It could, certainly, but anyone within six feet of the deceased when she was attacked would have received such a spray. And as I have already testified, there was a lot of blood in the bedchamber.'

'Is there anything else you can tell the court?'

'I don't believe so, Your Lordship.'

'Very well, thank you. You are now free to attend your patients.'

As Morton stepped back into the crowd, Fairbanks looked at both Sheriff Drury and Edward. 'Are there any more witnesses, or may I address the jury?'

When both men shook their heads, Fairbanks turned his attention to the twelve men on the bench. 'Before I address you on the task that confronts you, would one of you undertake to speak for the others when it comes to returning your verdict?'

After a hasty exchange, local baker James Flewitt emerged as their representative, and Fairbanks nodded. 'Thank you. Now please pay close attention, because what I have to say is addressed to you all.'

Twelve pairs of eyes fixed on his face as he began his address, as a court official called for total silence.

'Gentlemen, to you falls the solemn duty of deciding whether the prisoner before you, Francis Barton, is guilty of the murder of Agnes Timberlake. Before you may say positively that he is, you must have no doubt left in your mind that this is the case. Some judges, like myself, have taken to referring to what they call a "reasonable" doubt, but my experience has been that this only serves to confuse. Rather, think of it in terms of a "nagging" doubt, a bit like a toothache that refuses to go away. If you were to declare him guilty, then walk from here back to your homes with an uncomfortable belief that you might have got it wrong, then that would be the sort of doubt that should prevent you from finding him guilty.

'The facts are, you may think, evenly divided on either side. It is not, as I understand it, in dispute that Agnes Timberlake was murdered as she lay in her bed, alongside the prisoner. The question for you must be to identity whether or not Francis Barton murdered her. The evidence that you heard from the witnesses called against the prisoner, strongly suggested that the lady was killed with a sword by the prisoner, who had gone up to the bedchamber in her company. He was found in the chamber with her, covered in blood but otherwise unharmed, at a time when all the house doors were locked from the inside.

'But you have also heard evidence which may suggest to you that someone else entered the house while both the deceased and the prisoner were lying insensible from the effects of a powerful sleeping draught that had been introduced into the wine they had been drinking. That person may have been allowed into the house when the serving girl Mary Blythe — who also admitted to having stirred a substance into the wine — opened the door that gave access to the house from the adjoining workshop.

'You have also had the benefit of evidence from a physician who is of the belief that a chisel taken from that workshop is more likely to have caused the fatal wounds than a sword blade, and that had the weapon used been the prisoner's sword, then he would have expected it to display more evidence of its having been so employed.

'As you reach your conclusion, please bear in mind that you are not being asked to declare who murdered Agnes Timberlake — simply whether or not the prisoner Francis Barton did so. You may take a few moments while you ask yourself, before God, whether any doubt has entered your mind regarding the guilt of the prisoner, or you may withdraw to a room to the rear of this one in order to discuss the matter at greater length. Now, unless you have any questions that you wish to put to me, you must begin your deliberations.'

The twelve men took to muttering among themselves, and Edward's hopes rose as he saw several heads being shaken. After only a few minutes, as the judge sat writing on a parchment in front of him, dipping the quill at regular intervals into an ink pot set into the bench, James Flewitt rose to his feet and coughed politely to gain the judge's attention.

'Yes?' Fairbanks asked. 'Do you need more time in which to withdraw to consider the matter?'

'No, sir,' Flewitt replied. 'We don't think 'e done it.'

'You mean you have a reasonable doubt regarding the prisoner's guilt?'

'Aye, we do.'

'And that is the finding of you all?'

'Aye, it is.'

'Very well.' Fairbanks transferred his gaze to the prisoner. 'Francis Barton, you have been found, by a jury of your peers, to be not guilty of the murder of Agnes Timberlake. You are free to leave this court without a stain on your character. I would like to take this opportunity to congratulate the jury on having reached what I regard as the only appropriate conclusion in this case. Unshackle the prisoner, please, and let us all be about our dinner.'

14

Edward was the first to race over to congratulate Francis once the shackles had been removed from his wrists and he had been allowed to step from the dock out into the court.

Francis grinned as he embraced Edward. 'Thank you for your efforts on my behalf, Edward. You and the girl Mary, too, who took such a risk in stepping forward to tell the truth.' He looked over Edward's shoulder, where Sheriff Drury stood looking a little uncomfortable but with a small smile. 'Thank you to everyone who stood by me in my time of greatest need.'

'You are welcome,' Drury replied, 'but you start back about your duties tomorrow.'

'What would have happened to this excellent lamb roast had I been found guilty?' Francis enquired that evening as he carved another slice from the joint in the centre of the table.

Edward thought for a moment before replying, 'I would probably have sought to choke myself to death on it. As you will if you consume much more.'

'You have clearly never had to exist for a month on stale bread and Leen river water. But why are we dining alone? Where are Elizabeth and Margaret?'

'Safely installed with Elizabeth's parents in Ashby, where they will remain until this matter is resolved.'

'Your meaning?'

'The fact that a jury has determined that you did not murder Agnes does not take us any further forward in learning who *did*,' Edward reminded him. 'Surely, as one who loved her, you wish to learn the identity of her killer?'

'The man Sly, surely?'

'We do not know that. He may well swing for his attack on Mary, if not the long string of burglaries he was involved in, but Mary cannot be certain that it was he who she admitted into the house. And whoever did the deed did not do so for motives of their own; someone put them up to it, and I am resolved to discover who it was, and why.'

'Agnes's death is a town matter, is it not?'

'Indeed it is, and although I am no longer authorised to investigate it, *you* are, and I cannot believe for one moment that you will rest before you have done justice to Agnes's memory.'

'I certainly will not, but I would benefit from your assistance, Edward, given that you have taken the investigation to such an advanced stage. My concern is that you have already neglected your own duties in my interests, and that were I to encourage you to continue to do so, you would incur the wrath of your own sheriff.'

'Perhaps we can assist each other,' Edward mused. 'I need your constables to join with mine in order to investigate a barn in Derbyshire where I believe that the stolen items may be stored ahead of their sale. I have also received intelligence from Mary Blythe that leads me to believe that the person controlling the entire operation is someone of substance here in the town.'

'So we combine both our resources and our duties?'

'Have we not done so in the past, to considerable effect?'

'That was when we both served different sheriffs. How do we know that our current masters will be so agreeable to such an arrangement?'

'We will not know until we ask them, so I suggest that we do not. The successful outcomes will be the only justification that we will require.'

Francis nodded, though the expression on his face was solemn. 'Do you still believe that Thomas Timberlake murdered his own mother?'

'Not any longer,' Edward conceded. 'For one thing, had he been the person who prevailed upon Mary to drug your wine, she would have told me. And for another he had no need for her to open the workshop for him, since he had his own key. Furthermore, I do not believe that he had either the available finance or the will to hire the man who did it. Which leads me to believe that our two matters are related. Whoever commissioned the murder already enjoyed the services of the band of cut-throats with whom Henry Sly and Mary Blythe were associated. Mary has left me in no doubt that these are the same men who are responsible for the spate of recent burglaries.'

'And who do you believe to be the man of substance in command of these burglars, and by inference the man behind the murder of Agnes, to be?'

Edward looked thoughtful for a moment. 'I was for some time confused by the conflict in accounts between Thomas Timberlake and Josiah Greenwood for the reason they met on the day Agnes died. According to Greenwood, Thomas sought his accommodation in the repayment of a somewhat modest debt to a man called Daniel Gabriel. This strikes me as inherently unlikely, since the amount in question could be acquired by the simple expedient of a quick sale of one of his sculptures. Thomas, on the other hand, claimed that Greenwood wished to alert him to what he alleged was the embezzlement by yourself of the entire sum loaned to you by Agnes. Apart from the fact that this would not be a legally accurate description of your supposed actions, it served three purposes. The first was to explain away what I suspect is the complete absence of Agnes's gold in Greenwood's vault. The second was that it kept Thomas away from the house while his mother was being done to death. And the third was to divert suspicion towards you, and convince Thomas of your guilt.'

'So you suspect Greenwood?'

'The evidence points his way. It would also explain why Thomas arrived home earlier than anticipated that afternoon. He raced to his mother's house, determined to put you to the question regarding his inheritance, thereby disturbing the two men sent there.'

'So how do we set about finding evidence against Greenwood?' Francis asked as he absorbed this information.

'We break up this gang of burglars, who will reveal the identity of the man who was paying them handsomely for their labours. If, as I believe, the burglaries and the murder are linked, then we solve both mysteries at once.'

Francis raised his beer mug across the remains of the lamb roast. 'Here's to an advantageous partnership. Tonight I shall enjoy the luxury of sleeping in my own bed, but tomorrow I shall cross Whitefriars Lane for breakfast with you, before we set out on our quest.'

'And here's to justice,' Edward added as they clinked mugs.

Edward was still in bed when there came a knock on his bedchamber door.

Robbie Bishop poked his head round the door. 'Sorry to wake you, Master, only Bailiff Barton's arrived, and Meg says that breakfast will be on the table as soon as you get your clothes on. Mary's made you some special cheese sauce to dip your bread in, and it tastes right delicious.'

Edward quickly dressed and descended the staircase, bleary-eyed. He took a seat at the table opposite Francis, who was already eating ravenously. 'Quite like old times,' he muttered, referring to the days when he and Francis had shared the house across the road in Whitefriars Lane. 'I get up only to find that you've disposed of most of the breakfast.'

'I learned, during my days in confinement, to eat what I could, when I could,' Francis grinned at him with a mouthful of manchet loaf. 'And you would appear to have two of the best cooks in town.'

Edward smiled as he reached across the table and tore off some of the loaf, which he dipped into the cheese dish. It was good to see his friend had regained his appetite. 'Why the early start?' he asked.

'I thought we might gather the troops ahead of our proposed journey into Derbyshire,' Francis replied. 'I can have my constables ready by dinner time, whereas you, I suspect, will need to travel across half the county to round up yours.'

'When do you propose that we travel?'

'The day after tomorrow, perhaps.'

Edward thought for a moment. 'When I need to assemble all the county constables, I normally send word for them to meet me at Wollaton. But I can hardly do so without alerting Sheriff Willoughby to our plans, and he will not be best pleased to find that I am taking the county's officers into Derbyshire.'

'I thought you said that we were investigating burglaries in the county? Surely Sheriff Willoughby will be glad to learn that we are doing so jointly, and that we have such a fine body of men assembled for the task?'

'You don't know him as well as I do,' Edward grumbled. 'He is not easily pleased.'

Francis shook his head. 'But can you have your men assembled the day after tomorrow? That will be Thursday, will it not? My sense of time was somewhat diminished when all that I had to measure it by was the angle of the sun's shadow through my cell window.'

'At least you *had* a window, thanks to my generosity. Master Sly has no such luxury in his stink-pit under the Guildhall.'

Francis's expression hardened. 'If I were able to get my hands on him,' he snarled, 'I would soon put an end to his misery. Thanks to him I have lost over a month of my life, not to mention the only woman I have ever truly loved.'

'We cannot be certain that Sly killed Agnes,' Edward reminded him, 'and thus far he has declined to tell me who did. At least, he mentioned a man called Job Manners, but something about the alacrity with which he said it makes me suspicious.'

Francis sighed heavily. 'But we digress. Can you be ready by Thursday?'

'Probably, but you can explain matters to Sheriff Willoughby. If it comes to that, will not your own sheriff look askance at your removal of all the constables from the town?'

'I intend to leave a few behind on double duties,' Francis explained. 'They will not complain if the alternative is a two-day ride into Derbyshire, then a two-day ride back.'

'We will need to secure the necessary provisions. I doubt that Sir Francis will be graciously inclined to allow me to raid his larder for that purpose, so we might each agree to assume responsibility for the provisioning of our own men. I might prevail upon Meg and Mary to bake enough bread, but I fear that I will need to sweet-talk the Wollaton Hall cook into parting with supplies of cheese and salted fish.'

'I know enough merchants in town who owe me favours to ensure that my men will be well fed,' Francis replied. 'Although I shall need to inspect the supplies in order to determine their age. An outbreak of the flux is the last thing we need during an enforced march.'

The sun was high on Thursday as Edward stood nervously alongside Francis on the front steps of Wollaton Hall, watching as county constables arrived on horseback from their various villages. Edward could expect as many as ten in all, whilst lying around on the grassy greensward in front of the Hall were the same number from Francis's town contingent. Willoughby was currently out inspecting his coalmine, and it was hoped that he would not choose this moment to return and witness half his larder being loaded onto one of his coal wagons and one of his carters being pressed into service.

'Will you address the troops, or shall I?' Edward asked.

'This is your expedition,' replied Francis, 'so I shall not steal your thunder.'

Some of the men began to scramble to their feet as Edward walked down the steps towards them, but he waved his arm in a gesture that they should remain as they were.

'As you may already have learned,' he shouted, in order to be heard by them all, 'we will be crossing the county boundary into Derbyshire in order to locate the property stolen in recent weeks from various wealthy houses across the county. I believe I know where it may be found, and if I am correct then I shall leave some of you men there to guard it while the rest return here for more wagons. Any questions thus far?'

'What authority do we have in Derbyshire?' asked Constable Dewhurst from Arnold.

Edward tapped his sword hilt. 'We shall be carrying our authority at our belts. The men we are seeking are skilful thieves, so I do not propose that we present written introductions when — and if — we engage such men as we may encounter when we get there.'

'Why aren't you using Derbyshire constables?' asked Constable Hedley, whose jurisdiction was Carlton.

Edward smiled grimly. 'The last Derbyshire constable I encountered betrayed me, so you will forgive me if I lack confidence in your Derbyshire colleagues.'

There appeared to be no more questions and so Edward ordered the men into two detachments, one from the county and the other from the town, to ride down the long straight drive that led north into the local village. He took up a position at the head of the twenty or so horse-born constables, with Francis alongside him and the wagon bringing up the rear, loaded with provisions for five days.

Heaving a sigh of relief as they cleared both the village and the entrance to the coalmine without encountering Willoughby, Edward tried to recall from his memory the various landmarks that he would need to look out for if they were to locate the barn that Mary had identified as the place where the stolen property was stored.

It was beginning to get dark as they came in sight of the lake just east of Nuthall, where he and Mary had spent a cramped night inside the boathouse. After stopping to refresh themselves at the water's edge, Edward's memory obligingly supplied a vision of a large wooded area a few miles further on and by the time it was fully dark, each of their horses was securely tied to a tree. It was now simply a matter of ensuring an orderly distribution of their supplies from the wagon, and instructing the men to get such sleep as they were able.

'Are we making good time?' Francis asked Edward as they lay under a spreading oak.

'So far as I can recall,' Edward told him. 'But you must appreciate that the last time I took this road I did so by night, and in the opposite direction.'

'Think you that we shall find the place we are seeking tomorrow?'

'I have every hope that we shall, but we will need to employ stealth once we reach it. I cannot hope that such a store of valuables will have been left unguarded and it would be my suggestion that we creep as close to it as we can get in the trees that surround it, then charge it as if it were an enemy citadel.'

'We shall follow your lead,' Francis said, smiling, 'but now let us at least attempt to sleep.'

As soon as the pale dawn began to show itself between the overhanging bows, Edward roused the men and led them out of the wood and onto the country track that would eventually lead to Matlock. He knew that the place they were seeking was only an hour or two east of Matlock, if only he could remember the name of the village through which they'd ridden before Mary had led the way into the wood.

Then his heart skipped as he saw a milestone which displayed the name Wessington. The name seemed familiar. Then he recalled that it had been shortly after leaving Wessington that he and Mary had taken the detour down the forest road to the barn of stolen goods, and shortly after that when they'd bedded down in a wooded hollow to hide through their first day.

He called a halt by raising one arm in the air and looked around him. Then he nudged his horse into the woodland, inside which he was fairly sure he had located the hollow in question. Francis sidled his mount alongside his and asked, 'Seeking out wild flowers, are we?'

'No,' Edward replied absently, 'but if my memory serves me well, this was where Mary and I hid during our retreat from Matlock. That being the case, then the track that leads to the barn lies only a little further ahead. Let's get back to the men before it gets dark. I propose that we let them rest and feed here before I go ahead in order to locate our target.'

'We may *all* rest and feed,' Francis agreed. 'But when you go in search of this barn of riches you will not be going alone.'

Edward shook his head. 'I need you to stay behind and lead the men, should I come to harm.'

'You are not seriously suggesting that you attack the place single-handed?'

'Of course not. I shall merely creep up on it, to ensure that it is as I remember it, then I shall return and collect the rest of you, ahead of a night attack.'

'So there will be no danger to you?'

'Did I not just say so?'

'Therefore there will be no danger to me either, when I accompany you,' Francis insisted.

Edward turned to him. 'In that case, I hope that you will also accompany me when I seek to explain to Sheriff Willoughby why I took all his constables, half his larder, one of his coal wagons *and* its driver for a jaunt in the Derbyshire countryside.'

'As you yourself observed when we first planned this scheme,' Francis said, 'the discovery of all these stolen goods will be explanation enough. So lead on, but only after we have fed.'

The sun was sinking fast, its last rays filtering through the canopy of oak, elm and birch under which Edward and Francis rode. Edward gave a small cry of delight as he recognised a track to his right that looked familiar. He turned his horse down it and with Francis alongside him he wound his way cautiously down the track to the point at which the forest ended, where he had previously gazed at a large barn.

It was no longer there.

Edward gave a curse and dismounted, as Francis slipped from his own saddle to stand next to him. After a lengthy silence, Francis said, 'You appear to have lost a barn.'

'The villains must have somehow transported it elsewhere,' Edward muttered in disbelief. 'Either that or I have the wrong location.'

Francis squinted, his eyes scanning the field before them. 'Unless my eyesight grows as old as my limbs some mornings, there is a patch of ground ahead that is darker than the rest. Could it be that your barn has not been transported, but has in fact been burned to the ground?'

'The result will be the same, and I have led twenty men on a fruitless mission,' Edward groaned.

'Twenty-one, strictly speaking,' Francis said. 'But let us investigate further.'

They crossed the coarse grass and quickly confirmed that Francis's eyes had not been failing him. There was a large rectangle of burned earth and assorted debris where the barn had stood little more than a week previously. Someone must have realised that the treasure store had been discovered and had taken urgent steps to empty it of its contents prior to burning it down. The only potential lead that Edward had possessed, and the only justification for the resources he had commandeered, was now a charred mark on the ground. He cursed loudly as he kicked at what was left.

Edward and Francis looked at each other in surprise as a clinking noise rose up from the debris and Edward reached down to enquire as to its origins.

'The ground is still warm,' he told Francis. 'But they left something behind in their eagerness to depart.' He brushed away the ashes and peered down at what lay beneath. 'All is not lost,' he muttered as he picked up a dish of some sort, and blew the white ash from it.

Francis also bent down, coming back up with a candlestick holder. 'At least we can light our own way home.'

'That's silver!' Edward exclaimed. 'And so is this dish. Let's retrieve what we can from this bonfire and take it back with us.'

'To what avail?' Francis asked.

'I can take what we recover back to those who were burgled, in proof that we did indeed locate where the loot had been hidden.'

'And the rest of it?'

'Will have to wait for another time,' Edward replied as he collected several more small items from beneath his feet, and loaded them into the pannier on his horse's flank. Then they turned back the way they had come.

Later that night, Edward and Francis lay down by a gurgling stream where they had made their bed for the night. They had told the men that they would return to Nottingham the following morning.

'So tell me, what ploy have you in mind for locating the rest of the stolen property?' Francis asked in the moonlight.

'We enquire of Henry Sly,' Edward suggested.

'Presumably *before* I kill him?' Francis responded. To his surprise, Edward didn't immediately express any horror at the suggestion.

'No — after you *threaten* to kill him. You have cause enough, and he is lying friendless in a cell. He wouldn't be the first to die down there, and who would mourn his passing?'

'You actually *want* me to run him through?'

'No, of course not. I just want him to *think* that you will and therefore provide us with further information,' Edward explained. 'This is what I propose. We both go to his cell, you threaten him with revenge for the death of Agnes, then I step in and offer to preserve his life in exchange for information regarding the true identity of Agnes's murderer and where we might find the stolen loot. There must be some place to which prospective customers are directed in order to examine what is available for purchase, and a barn in the middle of nowhere is hardly appropriate. For one thing, it might alert any genuine purchaser to the possibility that the items are stolen, and for another, it is not the sort of place in which wealthy gentlemen are accustomed to being entertained. There must therefore be another place — perhaps a fine house somewhere — in which sales may be effected, and I believe that Master Sly may choose to bargain for his life by advising us where that is located.'

'And if he is Agnes's murderer? *Then* can I kill him?'

'With me as a witness?'

'You would not betray me, surely?'

'As I understand matters,' Edward replied calmly, 'I owed you a debt of gratitude for your action in killing the man who murdered my mother in Quorndon. I did not enquire as to the circumstances in which that came about, nor do I intend to. I have since balanced the ledger by securing the evidence that took a hangman's noose from around your neck. Your next killing will either be for lawful cause, or I shall be obliged to give testimony against you.'

'Your honourable and law-abiding nature does you credit, Edward Mountsorrel,' came Francis' voice in the darkness. 'But one day it may make Elizabeth a widow before her time.'

15

The sun reflected brightly off the glasshouses next to the house in Chilwell as Edward dismounted from his horse. He was in the process of unclasping a sack from the side of his saddle when the steward came to the door and requested to know his business.

'I am here to see Master Holgate. I hope that he may be able to identify some items which we found recently in Derbyshire,' Edward told him, and was invited inside.

Two minutes later Edward was admitted into the drawing room, where Richard Holgate gingerly tipped the contents of the sack onto the floorboards in front of the empty fireplace. 'This silver candlestick may well be mine!' he exclaimed as he took a rag and rubbed the ash from it. 'Certainly I had one like it, part of a set that I bought from a dealer in Antwerp. Thank the Lord that it appears to be otherwise undamaged, but how does it come to be in this condition?'

'The robbers took fright when they somehow learned that their hiding place had been discovered,' Edward explained. 'They fled with the majority of the stolen items, then set fire to the barn in which they had been hidden. They must have overlooked these items in their rush to leave. Can you lay claim to any of the other items?'

Holgate lifted an eyeglass that hung from a string around his neck and inspected the remaining items. He gave a cry of delight.

'That silver plate is not mine, and neither is the serving cup, but you have found one of my favourite pottery items from Cathay! It was one of a series of six, each of the same design

— see here, isn't the workmanship sublime?' He rubbed the small vase carefully, holding it out for Edward to admire.

As Edward looked at it, he frowned. 'I have seen this before,' he told Holgate. 'Or at least, one of its fellows. Are they in common circulation?'

'Far from it,' Holgate told him. 'I doubt if there are any others here in England, since I acquired this particular set from a merchant in Amsterdam. If you have seen its like somewhere, then it must be another of those that were stolen from me — one from the same set!'

Edward stared again at the delicate image of a tall thin house set among willow trees, and summoned all his mental powers to recall where he had seen it before. Then he remembered, and he knew what it was about Josiah Greenwood's chamber that had seemed curious at the time. The man had been using an identical ornament as a paperweight, and had drawn attention to it when seeking to hold down parchments on his desk when a sudden draught of air had threatened to blow them off!

'Do you know a town merchant called Josiah Greenwood?' Edward asked.

Holgate shrugged. 'I know *of* him, naturally, since he is said to be most accommodating in the matter of secure storage of other peoples' wealth, but I have never had direct dealings with him.'

'So you would not perhaps have sold, or loaned, an object like this to him?'

'Of course not. These Cathay flower vases were the most precious within my collection and were kept safe in a cabinet in my display room. They disappeared — along with the cabinet itself — on the night that we were robbed. Why do you ask?

Have you seen one of them recently in the possession of this man Greenwood?'

'I have indeed,' Edward confirmed, as he considered the implications of what he had just learned. 'Would you be prepared to visit Greenwood's office, with a view to identifying a particular object?'

'Of course, and I would be eternally grateful to you if such an action might reveal the whereabouts of the remainder of my collection.'

'Then I shall return within a few days,' Edward assured Holgate as he rose to leave, 'and together we shall journey into town.'

The cell door crashed open and a red-faced Francis Barton appeared in the doorway, his sword drawn. Henry Sly gave a terrified whimper and scuttled backwards into the corner of his cell, his eyes fixed on the blade.

'You're finally going to get what's coming to you, you bastard!' Francis hissed as he advanced menacingly on his prey. 'You murdered the love of my life while I lay next to her. Your only mistake was not killing me along with her. I'm here to exact vengeance in her name!'

'Mercy!' Sly croaked as he put his hands in front of his face.

'I'll show you the same mercy you showed Agnes Timberlake!' Francis stepped forward with his sword arm raised. 'At least she was senseless when you killed her, but *you* will feel every agonising thrust of this blade.'

Sly's pleas were drowned out by a commanding shout from the doorway.

'Hold your hand!' ordered Edward. 'This is no way to enforce the queen's peace!'

Francis turned and glared at Edward. 'This is a town matter, and your authority runs only in the county. Avert your eyes while I enforce my own justice!'

'I am sworn to uphold justice wherever it is required,' Edward said, 'and I will not stand by and watch while you do to death a man who can give me valuable information regarding matters into which I am enquiring. Your quarrel with this man came to an end when the jury acquitted you.'

'It will *never* come to an end until he is dead!' Francis roared. 'He killed Agnes!'

'It weren't me — it were Robert Shadley!' Sly shouted.

Francis lowered his sword. 'Where is your proof of that? You were admitted to the house on the day that Agnes died — Mary Blythe has already told us that, so you must have killed her.'

'There was two of us!' Sly exclaimed. 'I kept the apprentice busy while Robert went in to do what we'd been paid for! It was him who went in when Mary opened the door, honest it was!'

'The last time I was here, you named the man as Job Manners,' Edward reminded him. 'Why are you now saying that his name was Robert Shadley?'

'You didn't have a sword then, threatening me,' Sly replied hoarsely. 'This time it's the honest truth, else God strike me dead — unless he does first,' he added, with a fearful look at the weapon in Francis's hand.

'So where might we find this Robert Shadley?' Edward asked. 'If we can run him to earth, then Bailiff Barton here will have a more worthy target for his blade.'

'You'll find him in Derbyshire, along with the rest of them,' Sly explained, as a faint hope of salvation began to show in his face.

'Derbyshire's a big county,' Edward said. 'If I am to ensure that my colleague here does not run you through, then you will need to supply clearer directions.'

'There's a house in Chesterfield,' Sly blurted. 'It's a big house where we stored some of the stolen stuff and where we hid when we weren't robbing places.'

'I'm sure there are lots of big houses in Chesterfield,' Edward replied, 'and you aren't being of much assistance to me. Perhaps I should let Bailiff Barton do what he came here intent on doing.'

'No, please!' Sly pleaded. 'It's a merchant house in the town square, painted red and white. The man who runs it is called Pinkney — he's the one you need to see if you want to buy anything.'

'So, if we were to locate this house in Chesterfield that you describe, we'd not only find stolen goods, but also this man Shadley, who you claim murdered Agnes Timberlake?' Edward asked.

Sly nodded eagerly. 'But some of the stuff may've been sold since, you understand? There were folks coming and going from the house all the time.'

'And this man Pinkney, he is the one who organised all these robberies?'

'Yes and no. He's certainly the man who organises the viewings in Chesterfield, but then you have to pay a fellow here in town before you can collect it.'

'And who is this fellow?'

'Dunno — we were never allowed to meet him. Robert Shadley collected our money from him, and we just called him "Himself". I reckon that he's a wealthy man around the town, but I never got to know who he is.'

'He's messing us around!' Francis snapped.

Edward stared hard at Sly. 'How can we be sure that you've told us the truth?'

'Honest!' Sly insisted. 'Go to Chesterfield and find out for yourselves.'

'We might do that, Master Sly,' Edward replied as he led Francis out of the cell, slamming the door shut behind them.

Back upstairs, Edward punched Francis playfully on the shoulder. 'You see, there is more than one way to skin a cat.'

Francis looked back at him. 'My opinion of your ability to investigate wrongdoing just went up in equal proportion to my opinion of you as a man of moral integrity just went down.'

Edward introduced Richard Holgate to Josiah Greenwood inside the latter's spacious business chamber two days later.

'This is Master Holgate, from Chilwell,' Edward said, in his best impersonation of a man of business. 'He recently suffered the loss of a great number of valuables in an overnight robbery of his house and is now desirous of finding a safe place in which to store what remains to him. Naturally I thought of you, although being an officer of the law rather than a merchant I thought it best if I simply effected the introduction.'

Greenwood's reply was guarded. 'It would naturally depend upon the size and number of such items as you wish to store,' he told Holgate. 'My vaults are obviously of limited capacity and in the main they are used only to store smaller items of value, such as coins and gold.'

'The items I have in mind are in the main very small,' Holgate replied, stern-faced. 'They consist of rich ornaments acquired during my frequent journeys across the Channel, principally to the Low Countries. For example, that ornate vase on your desk is very close in appearance to one of a set of six that I purchased late last year from a dealer in Amsterdam. In fact, unless I am very much mistaken, it is indeed one from that very set. If I might examine its underside for the maker's distinctive mark?'

He held out a hand in anticipation of being handed the item, instead of which Greenwood lifted it swiftly from his desk and held it close to him, as if defending it from theft.

'You must be mistaken, sir. This came into my possession some years ago, as a gift from a friend who I had accommodated in the matter of safe storage of some items.'

'No doubt this friend can confirm the circumstances of your coming into possession of it,' Edward suggested icily. 'His identity, if you would be so good?'

'He is a personal friend!' Greenwood protested. 'I could not betray a confidence in such a manner.'

'Betray him with regard to *what*, exactly?' Edward persisted. 'Your words suggest that the item was indeed stolen, and since you are found to be in possession of it, the suspicion of its theft falls upon you. But if, as you claim, it came from a friend, then the simple disclosure of that friend's identity would assist in clearing your own name of any such suspicion.'

Greenwood hesitated for a moment, then he whispered, 'Daniel Gabriel.'

'Master Gabriel, the moneylender?' Edward asked. 'I was not aware that he was a collector of porcelain. We shall of course make enquiry of him in due course, but in the meantime I require you to hand over the item in question. I shall of course give you a receipt for it.'

Back outside Greenwood's premises in Goose Gate, Edward handed the vase over to Holgate, who thanked Edward profusely for his assistance in reclaiming it.

'Do you think he has the remainder of my property hidden in his vaults?' he asked.

Edward shook his head. 'He would not be so incautious, although clearly he could not resist showing off that beautiful vase. And you heard his explanation — he all but blamed the robberies on Daniel Gabriel.'

'Do you believe him?'

'No more than I believe certain other things that he told me during a previous meeting regarding the murder of Agnes Timberlake.'

'So where do you believe that my remaining property may be located?'

'If it has not already been resold to eager purchasers, then I believe it to be currently lying in a certain house in Chesterfield. If you are agreeable, then I would appreciate your assistance in a ruse designed to test that belief.'

'I am convinced that *you* could lie your way through your part in any such scheme,' Francis grinned as he and Edward sat down to a hearty supper at Edward's house. Meg served them wine while Mary placed more loaded platters on the table. Mary then stepped back against the wall, awaiting further instructions. 'But what you propose would involve others who are perhaps not so gifted.'

'You need not worry,' said Edward. 'They will each be playing themselves, with one exception — the manservant. Richard Holgate will approach the Chesterfield house posing as himself — a merchant seeking to acquire replacement items for the ones stolen from him.'

'Hold there,' Francis demanded as he pointed his meat knife in Edward's direction. 'Already there is a fundamental flaw in your scheme — Holgate will surely be recognised by those who robbed him, if your assumption regarding the nature of this house in Chesterfield is correct.'

Edward shook his head. 'The house was robbed at night, while Holgate and his servants were in their beds, and the robbery was not discovered until the following morning. It is unlikely that the robbers took the trouble to learn, in advance, of the name of the owner of the house they were plundering. And even if they did,' Edward continued, 'I shall be waiting outside the property with our constables, ready to make the necessary arrests at sword-point.'

'Will you be the one posing as Holgate's manservant?'

'When they know me by sight already?' Edward asked with raised eyebrows. 'You forget that a number of these villains took it upon themselves to poison my beer and truss me up like a turkey. Thanks to Mary I escaped, but they will surely not have forgotten my features in the short time that has elapsed since then.'

'Who, then, will be assuming the role of the manservant?'

'Who else but your good self?' Edward replied. 'And before you decline the opportunity, let us not lose sight of the fact that one of these oafs was probably responsible for Agnes's murder. Henry Sly named a man called Robert Shadley, did he not, and told us that he could most probably be found in the Chesterfield house?'

'In which case he will recognise *my* face from where I lay next to Agnes when he killed her,' Francis objected.

'The murderer would have been concentrating his entire attention on the foul deed he had to perform. You are far less likely to be recognised than I, and once we are inside, your true identity will be disclosed soon enough.'

'So who else will be a part of this ruse?' Francis asked dubiously.

'First of all, we shall need a carrier, if we are to persuade our quarry that we have come seeking items to purchase. I propose that we employ Thomas Bishop at his normal rate of hire, and of course travelling alongside him will be his labourer, and our good friend with the hammer fists — his own son Robbie.'

There was a sharp intake of breath from Mary, and she flushed when she realised that they were both staring in her direction.

'Sorry, Masters,' she muttered, 'but what you're planning sounds dangerous.'

'So it is, Mary,' Edward confirmed. 'But Robbie can defend himself, and no doubt his father will require his services.'

'Yes, to heave goods on and off his wagon, but you mentioned swords.'

'You need have no concern,' Edward told her, but her expression remained doubtful as she curtsied and rushed from the room.

'Well,' Francis observed as he watched Mary go. 'That's *one* of your players about to be dissuaded from the role he was about to play. Let us hope that your powers of persuasion are greater than Mary's.'

16

They halted a few hundred yards short of the town square in Chesterfield and took stock of their position. Edward and Francis slid from their saddles and watched as the last of their half dozen wagons rolled to a halt at the end of the line, each of them containing a handful of the constables they'd brought with them. Immediately behind them was the wagon that Thomas Bishop had been hired to bring. Alongside him sat his son Robbie, impatient for some physical action after spending two long days staring at the rump of the horse pulling their empty wagon, not to mention the uncomfortable night he'd spent sleeping underneath it with his father in a wood just north of Alfreton. Already the sun was high in the sky, and the constables were grumbling among themselves.

Edward and Francis were joined by Richard Holgate, who gazed around the busy square. 'It looks like market day,' he observed.

Edward nodded. 'All to the good. No-one will pay notice to the additional wagons and men. The men can stroll casually through the market, though not too far from our target, which by my judgment is that three-storeyed house across on the far side, red and white as described by Henry Sly. I'll position myself a few yards from the front door; the men must ensure that they can clearly see me when I give the signal.'

'What about the wagons?' Thomas Bishop asked.

Edward thought briefly. 'We'll leave them here — we won't need them until it comes to loading our prisoners. But we'll need your cart by the front door to begin with, maintaining the subterfuge that Master Holgate is here in order to purchase items, accompanied by his manservant. Thomas, I suggest that you stay with the cart, but let Robbie go in with Master Holgate and Bailiff Barton, since his brawn may come in useful should they need it before the constables arrive.'

'How will you and the men enter the house?' Francis asked.

Edward grinned. 'It would be nice if you were to open the door for us. Pretend that you're going to speak to your carter. Once I get the signal from you, I'll call the constables to my side and we'll storm the place.'

Looking less than happy with the arrangement, Francis accompanied Holgate and Robbie to the front door, where Holgate engaged the brass knocker several times. There was a lengthy delay before they heard bolts being drawn back from the inside, and the heavy oak door opened to reveal a suspicious pair of eyes over a full ginger beard.

Holgate took a deep breath. 'I wish to do business with Master Pinkney, should he be at home.'

'Wait there,' they were instructed, as the door was closed in their faces.

Holgate looked sideways at Francis. 'I hope this works,' he whispered nervously.

'If it doesn't, you can blame Bailiff Mountsorrel, since it was his hare-brained scheme,' Francis whispered back.

The door opened once more, and the same bearded face enquired as to their identities.

'I am Richard Holgate, agricultural merchant from Nottinghamshire, and these men are my employees. I wish to acquire new table plate, and I am advised that your master might be in a position to supply me with some of the finest.'

'Who sent you?' the doorman asked.

Holgate responded in a haughty tone. 'That is none of your concern. Now, is your master at home and prepared to receive us, or must I go elsewhere?'

'I am James Pinkney,' announced a florid-faced man who suddenly appeared from behind his surly doorkeeper, 'and as you have obviously been advised, I may be in a position to supply your needs. But prior to inviting you inside, I insist on knowing who sent you.'

'It were Josiah Greenwood, a merchant from the town,' Francis said in what he hoped was a passable imitation of a rough Nottingham brogue smoothed out over time into something appropriate for a male attendant employed by a wealthy tradesman.

'What led you to be speaking with this Master Greenwood, and how came he by the knowledge that I might have suitable goods for sale?'

'I sent my man Francis here to ask around town, among his many acquaintances, where we might search out high-quality merchandise,' Holgate replied. 'I must own that I was taken aback by the need to travel this far out of the town, and unless I am admitted with no more delay, I shall turn back the way I have come. Travelling the country tracks with so much wealth in one's possession is a hazardous undertaking at the best of times, and I do not take kindly to being held on your doorstep like a common tradesman.'

'Come in,' Pinkney said, the reference to wealth having apparently overcome his earlier reluctance. 'If you would care to pass down the hallway to the room at the end, you will find an impressive collection of superior items that I have available.'

They walked down to the room indicated, and Pinkney threw open the door to reveal what looked more like the overstocked audience chamber of a royal palace than a domestic hall.

Stacked from floor to ceiling was an eye-dazzling array of padded furnishings, behind which hung wall tapestries that would not have seemed out of place in a bishop's palace, most of them depicting Biblical scenes. Arranged on various tables were the finest collections of gold and silver plate that might be found anywhere in Europe, and Holgate's eyes opened in wonder as he surveyed the riches laid out before them.

'You mentioned table plate,' Pinkney reminded Holgate. 'As you can see, there is a vast range for your perusal. Once you have made your selection I will list it, and you may take the list back to Nottingham in order to make payment.'

'Can't I pay for it today and take it home with me?' Holgate asked. 'Must I make the journey a second time?'

'Those are my terms of business,' Pinkney confirmed. 'I am merely the custodian of the items that you see, which in truth are owned by a merchant in Nottingham who makes use of my premises. Once you have selected what you wish to purchase, I will write out a list and give you a note of the person to whom you must take it. Once you have made payment, the man in question will confirm payment with his seal, then send you back here with the list, at which time you may take it away, and not before.'

'How can I be sure that the items I choose will not be sold to others in the meantime?' Holgate asked suspiciously.

'The items will be consigned to a separate room, and held there for two weeks pending your return with the sealed list.'

'And you'll tell my master where to go in order to pay?' Francis asked in his assumed Nottingham accent.

Pinkney nodded. 'And now, feel free to make your selection, Master Holgate.'

Richard and Francis moved to a table in the centre of the hall that was piled high with silver and gold table plate, and Holgate began turning some of the silverware over to examine various marks on their underside. He gave a small hiss and whispered to Francis, 'Some of these are mine!'

'Go along with the pretence, in order that we may learn who in Nottingham is behind all this,' Francis instructed him and Holgate began to select items and place them to one side.

He turned back to Pinkney with a question. 'How much will these items cost me?'

'That will depend upon the owner, when you take the list to him,' Pinkney replied. 'I am no valuer, and a man of wealth such as yourself will surely have little concern over the cost.'

Holgate selected three more silver dinner plates then turned back to Pinkney.

'These should suffice; if you would be so good as to make out the list and advise me to whom I must make payment.'

Pinkney walked across to a desk in the corner of the room, from which he selected writing materials and began itemising the objects Holgate had selected. Once the ink had dried he handed it across to Holgate, who in turn passed it to Francis.

'Please go back outside and enquire of the carrier if he knows where this owner may be found,' Holgate instructed Francis with a small wink that was the cue to call in the others.

Francis gave a slight bow and turned to go, but Pinkney called him back.

'You will not leave until I say so!' he ordered in a stern tone that was in marked contrast to his earlier obsequiousness.

Francis tried to look suitably chastised, while Holgate once again rose to the challenge.

'How dare you order my servant about, sir!' he said in a suitably outraged tone. 'I simply wish to ensure that we have adequate directions before we depart.'

'There is not a person in Nottingham who does not know Master Gabriel,' Pinkney insisted, 'so I suggest that your carrier will need no instruction, and I am suspicious of why your servant should be so anxious to leave.'

'This you will discover when I return,' Francis replied ominously as he strode across the room and flung open the door, followed at his heels by Robbie, who until that moment had been a silent observer.

The opened door revealed the presence of two men in the narrow hallway, each armed with a drawn sword. Francis gave a wild yell as he drew his own weapon and leaped towards the first of them.

While they thrust and slashed at each other in a duelling dance that took them, step by step, towards the front door, Robbie made a dash down the hallway in order to flatten the other swordsman with a swinging haymaker punch that sent the man bouncing off the cedar-panelled wall and back onto Robbie's fist, which ended the man's resistance for the immediate future. Robbie then turned to the front door, wrenched it open and yelled for Edward.

Edward, for his part, turned with a loud shout and a raised arm, summoning the constables from their various places among the market stalls. They surged through the open front door and raced down the hallway and up the staircase, into every room in the house, dragging out everyone they could find inside.

The final haul was nine men, who were led outside, suitably bound and cursing, and thrown into the waiting wagons, to the considerable entertainment of those attending the local market.

'A good day's work, I suggest,' Edward remarked to Francis as he surveyed the scene. 'No doubt some of them will be prepared to earn their freedom by peaching on the rest.'

'I have learned two things of value,' Francis replied. 'The first is that the boy Bishop is handy with his fists, and as soon as we get back to town I'll recommend to the sheriff that we take him on as a constable.'

'That will certainly please Mary Blythe,' Edward nodded. 'And what is the second thing?'

'That you were correct in suspecting Daniel Gabriel,' Francis replied. 'It is he who lies at the centre of the spate of burglaries in the county.'

'But we only have Pinkney's word for it at present,' Edward pointed out. 'I think we will need to continue with our ruse.'

'In what manner?' Francis asked.

'Master Holgate is armed with a parchment that he is supposed to be taking to Gabriel in order to make payment. We need Holgate to present that parchment to Gabriel in order to confirm that he is indeed behind the robberies. And I still wish to locate Richard Grindley, the false constable from Matlock. He is not among those that we already have in custody.'

'You must pursue that matter separately,' Francis suggested. 'Our priority must be to get these oafs back to Nottingham, charged with burglary. And while you hunt down your Constable Grindley I will go in search of this man Robert Shadley, who Henry Sly assured us was the one who entered the house and killed poor Agnes. Anyway, let us about our business, and haul this lot off back to town. If you do not have sufficient space in the Shire Hall, I may be able to house a few of them in the cells underneath the Guildhall.'

'I cannot go with Richard Holgate to visit Daniel Gabriel,' Edward told Francis as they rode slowly at the head of the procession of wagons heading south-east towards Nottingham.

'He knows me to be the county bailiff, and was far from friendly during our last encounter.'

'Nor would he fail to recognise me as the town bailiff, I suspect,' Francis said. 'But we cannot allow Holgate to go there alone.'

'Perhaps you might wish to further test the mettle of the young man who you have in mind for a new constable?' Edward said. 'All we need is confirmation that Gabriel is prepared to take payment for the items that Holgate has selected, then we may enter and arrest him, taking with us such number of men as will be necessary in order to effect Gabriel's arrest, along with any who display resistance.'

'Will young Robbie be sufficient, do you think? You will be gambling with Holgate's life, will you not?'

'No doubt you are correct, but he doesn't know that, does he?'

'Although it is a town matter in form, it is county business in substance,' Francis insisted, 'and should it go awry I shall expect you to take the blame.'

Edward nodded. 'I have nothing to lose, given that I must already justify to Sir Francis why I took food from his larder, and a wagon and driver from his coal concern, not to mention my absence for the best part of a week.'

'Surely, when he learns that you have solved the matter of these burglaries, he will shower you with praise?'

'You clearly have little experience of Sir Francis,' Edward grinned. 'But I think that it's time to advise Holgate and Robbie of their next assignment, and get them back to Nottingham before word of today's events reaches Daniel Gabriel.'

'All you wish me to do is present this list of items to Master Gabriel, then walk over to the window?' Richard Holgate asked as he, Edward, Francis and Robbie stood in a tight group at the foot of Cow Lane, just around the corner from Daniel Gabriel's chambers in Long Row.

'That's correct,' Edward assured him. 'From memory, his main business chamber overlooks the Market Place, and even though it's not market day it's busy enough, and nobody's likely to notice either Francis or myself. So when you give the signal we'll just demand admission to the house and arrest him.'

'If for some reason you can't get to the window, then it will be sufficient if Robbie does so instead,' Francis added. 'Either one of you will suffice, and we'll lose no time in coming in after you.'

'Let's be off, then,' Robbie suggested eagerly, and he and Holgate walked around the corner towards the front door of Gabriel's business premises.

'I hope you can live with your conscience if this goes awry,' Francis muttered as he and Edward strolled casually into the Market Place, making a mental note of the many town and county constables who'd taken up innocuous-looking positions in various locations around the square. 'Holgate clearly has no knowledge of how Gabriel does business.'

'Holgate is eager to pay Gabriel back for the theft of his property, only some of which has so far been retrieved,' Edward replied. 'As for my conscience, my heart is beating fit to burst from my chest, so please don't remind me.'

They watched from a distance as Holgate and Robbie knocked on the door, then held their breath as the door opened and they disappeared inside.

Robbie and Richard Holgate were ushered reverently into Gabriel's business chamber once the nature of their business had been announced. Robbie looked casually to his right and confirmed that through the window he could see the activity in the busy Market Place, although he couldn't see either of the two bailiffs, which was perhaps as well. He turned his attention back to the conversation that was taking place.

'I have journeyed from Chesterfield,' Holgate announced, 'in order to secure the purchase of a quantity of silver plate that I saw on display at a house there. The merchant who showed it to me supplied me with this list, which I am assured you can price, then take my money and issue me with a receipt which I may then take back to Chesterfield in order to collect my purchase.'

'And who advised you that this might be possible?' Gabriel asked warily.

'The man named himself as Pinkney,' Holgate replied with mounting irritation in his voice. 'But surely the fact that I have this list, which I am assured is your normal, if somewhat unusual, way of doing business, means that you need enquire no further? I have never before in my many years of acquiring the finer objects for my household known of such a way of doing business as yours, and I would require little persuasion to cancel my interest in what you have for sale, and seek to fulfil my requirements elsewhere.'

'That will not be necessary,' Gabriel assured him calmly. 'However, purely for my own interest, I should like to know with whom I am dealing.'

'My name is Richard Holgate, and I reside in Chilwell, to the west of here, where because of my ample independent means I am able to indulge myself in agricultural experiment. Should you require references, I can supply them.'

'That will not be necessary. Pray, tell me, how did you come to learn of the house in Chesterfield?'

'I tasked my steward to make enquiry here in town, and he was advised of the existence of Master Pinkney's house.'

'By whom?'

'I have no idea. Now, are you able to accommodate me in the matter of this purchase, or must I take my leave?'

'You may be assured of two things, Master Holgate,' Gabriel replied in a low voice. 'The first is that you have come to the correct place in order to acquire your purchases, and the second is that you will leave here when I deem it appropriate. So you may tell your man over there to cease staring out of the window, as if deciding which pie stall to grace with his custom.'

'I do not believe that I find your manner to my liking, Master Gabriel,' Holgate replied. 'To the extent that I have resolved to take my money elsewhere.'

Gabriel picked up the bell on his desk and rang it urgently. The door behind his desk opened, and two men entered the room and advanced on Holgate and Robbie.

'Detain these two until I can determine their true identities,' Gabriel ordered.

Before the men could carry out the command, Robbie raced forward and knocked one of the burly men sideways with a blow to the side of his head. His companion drew his sword and Holgate ran for cover behind Gabriel's desk, just in time to hear a bellow of pain and see a sword drop from an arm that had just been rendered useless. Then came a crashing noise from the direction of the front door, and raised voices in the hallway outside.

It was an unequal contest as a dozen armed constables hurried past the shattered front door and made hasty work of subduing four men who stumbled from a room to the rear in which they had been drinking their way through a previously uneventful day. They were ordered, face down, onto the hall floor, and were secured at the wrists before being hauled outside and thrown into waiting wagons.

Edward and Francis rushed into the main room, where Robbie had his arm around Gabriel's throat. There were two men lying on the floor, and the expression on Holgate's face clearly betrayed the fact that this was an aspect of commercial life that was entirely novel to him.

'Pardon the intrusion, Master Gabriel,' Edward said, 'but I am arresting you for your part in organising a spate of burglaries in the adjoining county.'

'This is an outrage!' Gabriel croaked. 'And get this animal off me before I choke to death!'

'You may release him, Robbie,' Edward instructed, 'since I wish him to retain enough breath to make a full confession once we have him in custody.'

'I know not of what you accuse me,' Gabriel insisted, rubbing his neck, 'but you shall answer for this to the town sheriff, who is a personal friend of mine.'

'I had no idea that my employer moved in such low circles,' Francis sneered, just as Robbie shouted a warning.

Francis instinctively leapt out of the way as the man Robbie had previously knocked to the ground advanced on him, his sword held above his head in the classic preamble to a downward slice. As he did so, he drew his own sword with an agility borne of frequent practice.

His assailant lost his balance as he found himself swiping down on thin air, and was perfectly positioned to receive a direct thrust to the heart from Francis's blade. The man stared down in disbelief at the fountain of blood that spurted down his hose, before he collapsed in a heap on the carpet.

'Talking of employers,' Edward continued calmly, as if watching a man die was an everyday occurrence. 'How did you manage to pervert Constable Grindley from his duty?'

'Who?' Gabriel demanded.

Edward nodded down at the body on the carpet. 'Richard Grindley, Constable of Matlock in Derbyshire, where some of your band of burglars spent their idle hours when not engaged in plundering the houses of the wealthy. Or did you not know that you had recruited an officer of the law from Derbyshire?'

'You ignorant fool,' Gabriel replied. 'That man is — or rather *was* — Robert Shadley.'

'You employed this man, and his name was Robert Shadley?' Francis asked as he gave the corpse a vicious kick in the groin. 'And did you so employ him to murder Agnes Timberlake?'

'I knew him as Robert Shadley,' Gabriel confirmed, now seemingly more aware of the peril that he was in. 'But I employed him for no murder. He was simply a man of action who knew no fear, and who I loaned out from time to time to those who had need of such attributes.'

'Did you hire him out recently, along with another man called Henry Sly? And if so, to whom, and why?' Francis demanded, his face red with anger.

'I know not why,' Gabriel replied, his voice betraying his nervousness. 'But I can advise you that the man who hired them was Josiah Greenwood.'

Edward turned to Robbie. 'Take Master Gabriel down to the Shire Hall, there to be handed over to my senior turnkey. Francis and I have an overdue appointment with Master Greenwood.'

17

'Was it really necessary to call me all the way from Wollaton?' Sir Francis complained to Edward. Willoughby was seated beside Sheriff Drury in the latter's house in Wheeler Gate. 'I fail to see why you needed me here to report back on those town matters that so distracted you.'

'I owe my life to that distraction,' Francis said in Edward's defence, from his seat next to Edward, across the table from the two sheriffs. 'However, I was able to repay my debt in a small way by assisting in the arrest of a very troublesome gang of burglars. It was because this operation proved to be connected to the murder of Agnes Timberlake that we asked to be allowed to report to you both, in order to save time and effort.'

'Yours, or ours?' Willoughby grunted, but Edward was not to be deterred.

'Both, of course,' he replied. 'Francis is correct when he asserts that it was due to my efforts to secure his acquittal of the murder of Agnes Timberlake that I gained a valuable lead to the burglaries that had been plaguing some of the finer houses in the county.'

'I don't suppose I'll be allowed to return to my business interests until I hear all, so let's just get on with it,' Willoughby conceded.

'As I have already disclosed,' Edward began, 'my primary interest was in learning what I could regarding the events of the afternoon in which the Widow Timberlake was killed. I was advised by Francis that the only other person who had been present before the doors to the house were locked from the inside was her maid, a young woman called Mary Blythe. It seems that whoever committed the foul deed was either this servant, or — more likely — someone who had gained access to the house with Mary's assistance. Then, by curious coincidence, I was instructed to find a young lady missing from her Wollaton home whose name just happened to be Mary Blythe.

'She was believed to have journeyed into Derbyshire,' Edward continued, 'with an individual named Owen. When I went in search of her, I made the mistake of relying on the assistance of a Constable Richard Grindley in Matlock. He betrayed me to the villains. My wine was drugged and, rendered insensible, I was trussed up and locked away in a room at the local inn, with a view to learning what I knew about their nefarious activities. Of course, at that stage I knew nothing, but thanks to Mary Blythe I escaped. I brought her safely back to Wollaton, and in exchange she told me all she knew about the men that she'd become associated with, and of whom she was now in mortal fear. It soon became obvious that these men were the very burglars that I'd been seeking.'

'And of course you reported the betrayal of this Derbyshire constable to me,' Willoughby confirmed. 'I trust that you are now in a position to have him apprehended?'

'He is dead,' Francis interposed. 'I should know, since I killed him. But he went by another name.'

'Perhaps you should explain the background regarding Agnes's fortune,' Edward suggested.

Francis nodded. 'Agnes had been left a wealthy woman when her husband died, and the family alabaster carving business was continued by his son, Thomas. Unfortunately, Thomas squandered such income as he derived from the business in idle pursuits such as gambling on cock-fights. In order to supplement his lifestyle he was forever importuning his mother for advances on the money left to her, which she had placed for safe-keeping in the vaults of a local merchant called Josiah Greenwood.'

Drury frowned. 'The man currently in custody awaiting trial for Agnes's murder?'

Francis nodded. 'The very same. In an attempt to prevent Thomas from constantly requesting money of her, Agnes prevailed upon me to accept the entire sum — a total in excess of one thousand pounds — as a personal loan for the remainder of her lifetime. She knew she could trust me, and she hoped that I would prove firmer in my resolve to keep Thomas's hands off it, as indeed I did. For this reason, relations between myself and Thomas were strained, so much so that when his mother was murdered, he assumed that I had committed the deed in order to silence his mother, who had allegedly learned that I had absconded with the money.'

'Is the money still with Josiah Greenwood?' Drury asked.

Francis shook his head. 'No, it is not. As we have only recently learned ourselves, it was Greenwood himself who had embezzled the entire sum. Agnes had grown suspicious and had demanded an accounting. That is why he arranged for her to be murdered, and this is where it becomes complicated.'

'You mean it was simple *this* far?' Willoughby said with raised eyebrows.

'I made numerous enquiries into the events surrounding Agnes's death,' Edward said, taking up the thread, 'and learned that two men arrived at the Timberlake workshop shortly before the murder. While one of them kept the apprentice occupied, a second man was admitted into the house by Mary, who had let herself into the house with her own key to the back door and who then unlocked the adjoining workshop door. While interviewing the apprentice, I also located a chisel used in the business, and the physician who examined Agnes was able to confirm that such a tool was more likely to have caused the wounds on her body than Francis's sword, which had been crudely daubed with her blood, along with his hose, in order to make it appear to have been the murder weapon. I believe that the killer picked up the chisel from the workshop bench while the apprentice was distracted, and took it into the house with him.'

'You can well understand why I was obliged to have Bailiff Barton here charged with the murder,' Drury commented to Willoughby. 'Particularly since he was unable to account for what had transpired.'

'This was because Mary had slipped a simple of valerian into the wine consumed by Agnes and Francis before they adjourned to the bedchamber,' Edward explained. 'Valerian can induce a deep sleep, so both Francis and Agnes were insensible when the man who had been admitted to the house killed Agnes.'

'Is the servant Mary to be charged for her part in all this?' Drury demanded.

'I owe my life to her honest testimony at my trial,' Francis reminded the sheriff.

'And for my part I owe her a debt of gratitude for revealing the identities of the burglars,' Edward added. 'Not to mention the fact that she helped me escape the men in Derbyshire.'

'But what does any of this have to do with Daniel Gabriel?' Willoughby asked.

'His was the hand behind the burglaries.'

'A wealthy man such as he, needing to stage burglaries?' Willoughby protested.

Edward nodded. 'It was the secret to his wealth. But allow me to return to the part of our narrative that links the burglaries with the murder.'

'Pray do so, else we shall be here all day,' Willoughby grumbled.

'You will recall that when Mary Blythe went on the run, she was accompanied by a man named Owen. When I brought Mary back to my house for her own protection, this man — whose real name was Henry Sly — came after her. He was captured, thanks to the excellent work of a young man named Robert Bishop, and who I am delighted to say has now become a town constable. When questioned, Sly admitted to having been the man who distracted the apprentice in Thomas Timberlake's workshop while another man who he named as Robert Shadley was admitted to the house, where he murdered Agnes. Sly also revealed the existence of a house in Chesterfield in which the items stolen from the county house burglaries were being stored and held for sale by a man named Pinkney.'

'We have been able to restore most of the items to their grateful owners,' Willoughby informed Drury. 'And Master Pinkney awaits trial for receiving stolen goods.'

'This was due in no small regard to the assistance I received from Francis and the town constables,' Edward told him. 'And by means of a subterfuge — in which one of those grateful owners helped us — we learned that the spider at the centre of the web was none other than Daniel Gabriel. It seems that in addition to being an unscrupulous moneylender, he also enjoyed a lucrative income from selling on stolen property. He had kept his identity a secret from all involved and was simply known as "Himself". We therefore employed another ruse in order to prove his involvement, but while inside his house

Francis was attacked by a man who he was obliged to kill in self-defence. By another strange coincidence this man turned out to be not only the Robert Shadley that we were seeking for the murder of Agnes Timberlake, but also Richard Grindley — the corrupt Matlock constable to whom I have already referred. Whatever his true name, he is now dead, and unavailable for trial for the murder.'

'Clearly you are a great believer in coincidences,' Drury commented with a wry smile. 'But if this man Shadley, or whatever his name was, was one of Gabriel's burglars and bodyguards, why has Josiah Greenwood been charged with the murder of Agnes Timberlake?'

'Allow me,' Francis interposed. 'Greenwood was a good friend of Gabriel's, since the latter made frequent use of Greenwood's vault in order to hide his ill-gotten wealth. When Greenwood had need to dispose of Agnes, he sought the assistance of his friend Gabriel in supplying someone to carry out the deed. Shadley was a violent character who had no qualms in killing Agnes. He has already poisoned two dogs belonging to Master Middleton in Bramcote, and the town is well rid of him.'

'Where lies your evidence against Greenwood?' Drury asked.

Edward smiled. 'Gabriel was only too anxious to name him when it looked as if he was about to be charged with the murder himself, given his regular employment of Shadley. And I believe that this completes our report to you both.'

'You would appear to have discharged your duties adequately,' Willoughby conceded as he rose to leave. 'I suppose that you will be back in your office at Wollaton tomorrow?'

'No, by your leave,' Edward replied. 'I have certain family matters to attend to first.'

'As you wish.' Willoughby frowned. 'You have one daughter, do you not?'

'Indeed I do, and she is currently with her grandparents,' Edward told him.

'Think yourself blessed,' Willoughby muttered as he headed for the door. 'I have seven, and no grandparents upon whom to impose them. Good day to you all.'

'Well done — both of you,' Thomas Drury said as he too stood. 'Will you also be taking some time to rest, Francis?'

Francis shook his head. 'I wish to remain occupied while I continue to grieve for the loss of Agnes.'

'I thought you had abandoned us,' Elizabeth cried as she threw her arms around Edward. 'But at least you came back alive. Margaret can now say "Dada", but I don't know why she takes the trouble, because it's "Mama" who looks after her all the time.'

'How have you enjoyed your time here in Ashby?' he asked politely as Catherine Porter set about making dinner while Edwin went to fetch beer.

Elizabeth leaned close to whisper into Edward's ear. 'I grow tired of Mother's strictures on the correct way to bring up a child. She gives tedious advice on how to remedy Margaret's snuffles and restless sleeping.'

'So you won't be plaguing me to bring you back here for a while yet?'

Elizabeth shook her head. 'Not for a while. I think I prefer the empty house in Whitefriars Lane when you are away all day. At least then I am my own person, with only Meg to distract me.'

'That may soon change,' Edward said, 'since we shall have to give employment to Mary, at least until her delivery.'

'She is with child? Robbie's, I hope?'

'Indeed Robbie, who is now employed as a town constable. I promised that we would both host and pay for their wedding next month, before the child begins to show. In the meantime, Mary can help with sewing, cooking and baby-minding?' Edward suggested. 'This will give you a little more free time.'

'Free time to gaze out into the lane and wonder when you will return?'

'You knew of my trade before we were married. Mary will need to learn from you what it is to be married to a constable.'

'I shall tell her that it is the greatest ambition to which any woman can aspire, if you promise me that we can have more children in due course.'

'Why wait?' Edward smiled and kissed her cheek. 'I'm here now, and I feel the need to withdraw to our chamber.'

'I hope that you will wash first,' Elizabeth said and wrinkled her nose. 'You have become so closely associated with your horse that you share the same perfume.'

'And after I have washed?'

'Then I shall endeavour to get you all sweaty again,' Elizabeth replied with a smile.

A NOTE TO THE READER

Dear Reader,

Thank you for taking the time to read this third novel in the series about Edward Mountsorrel and his life as bailiff to the sheriff of Nottinghamshire. Most of the action is set in the town of my youth, Nottingham, and the delightful dales of Derbyshire to which I travelled on many weekends with my parents, courtesy of our 1950's motorcycle and sidecar.

In the year in which this novel is set — 1593 — Nottingham had a population of approximately 4,000 people. Although this seems laughably small by modern standards, it was sufficient to denote it as a substantial town, a market centre for the surrounding county. Many of the thoroughfares mentioned in the pages you have just read (for example Bridlesmith Gate, Goose Gate, Stoney Street and Wheeler Gate) still retain their original names, but are very different from how they would have looked like over four centuries ago.

Late sixteenth-century Nottingham was, as described by one of its most lyrical diarists, 'A Town in a Garden'. The streets were wide by the standards of the day, and were in the main lined with the brick and timber houses of the mercantile aristocracy — the wool merchants, butchers, furriers, alabaster sculptors and suchlike — intermingled with the town mansions of the minor nobility, the families who had ruled this Midland capital for generations. Almost every house, of necessity, had a garden, and the wealthier of them could also boast an orchard.

The necessity for a garden was dictated by practical considerations, for it was in the garden that one would find the kitchen, situated safely away from the main house because of the ever-present risk of fire. Somewhere in that garden could also be found, in most cases, what passed for the sanitary facilities, referred to colloquially at the time as the 'jakes' — an open cesspit surrounded by a sad structure designed to give privacy to those making use of it.

With wealth came political power, and the names of those appointed by the monarch to enforce law and order as 'sheriff' of either the town or the county (two separate jurisdictions) are a fascinating 'Who's Who' of privilege and class in those days. Whether they were born with a silver spoon in their mouth, or acquired eminence through astute commercial dealings, they were the 'Establishment' of their day, and their 'townhouses' were more like 'stately homes' within a network of broad leafy lanes.

With the privileges of rank came duty. The two bailiffs who feature in this story — Edward and Francis — both served men of high status, whose role as sheriff carried with it the responsibility for maintaining law and order for their jurisdictions, and 'presenting' defaulters for trial. Central to this novel is the accusation of murder faced by Francis Barton, and the criminal justice system to which he was subjected.

Before a man could be committed for trial before a Royal Justice in those days, it was necessary for him to be 'presented' for that purpose by a 'grand jury' made up of locals. The system of criminal trial in late Elizabethan England was partway through a transition from the 'old' system into the one that we observe today. Under the 'old' system the 'jury' members were selected on the basis that they knew something of the circumstances of the events that had led to the accused being on trial — to all intents and purposes they were also what we would today call the 'witnesses'. Under our modern laws we make great effort to ensure that those who sit in judgment have *no* such prior knowledge, and reach a decision of 'Guilty' or otherwise solely on the basis of what the independent, and unbiased, witnesses can tell them.

By 1593, the assizes to which Francis Barton was committed was lurching uncertainly between the old and the new system. It would, for example, be another three hundred years before the accused person was allowed to testify in their own defence, and whether or not they would be allowed to call witnesses in their cause would depend upon the whim of the trial judge commissioned to preside over the case, who varied alarmingly in both their ability and their sense of 'justice'. Even several generations later, the infamous Judge Jeffreys was not dismissed from office despite his enthusiasm in 'playing the system' in order to condemn to horrible deaths those who had supported the Monmouth Rebellion.

I was not therefore exaggerating in depicting Justice Fairbanks as being somewhat unusual in his humane approach to Francis's murder trial, and describing Edward's permission to adduce evidence favourable to Francis as something resembling a privilege. This was the way it was, warts and all, and Francis had God on his side that day.

I genuinely hope that this novel provided a few hours of pleasant diversion and a convincing step back in time. As ever, I would be delighted to see a review of it posted on **Amazon** or **Goodreads**. Alternatively, feel free to visit, and contact me on, my author website: **davidfieldauthor.com**.

Happy reading!

David

Sapere Books is an exciting new publisher of brilliant fiction and popular history.

To find out more about our latest releases and our monthly bargain books visit our website:
saperebooks.com

Printed in Great Britain
by Amazon

63359540R00107